Dream

A DRAGONS OF THE CROSSROADS PREQUEL

LORI SALTIS

VAGABOND TALES

Copyright © 2023 by Lori Saltis
ISBN: 9781967542062

Cover art by DAZED Designs

Published by Vagabond Tales.
All Rights Are Reserved.

To India Cale. Thank you for believing in my dreams.

Dream

GERRY

This dragon, he's a crazy bugger. He sleeps at the bottom of the sea, though he's not really sleeping. More like brooding – the morose bastard. When he's not doing that, he's moving through the water, undulating like a snake, scattering schools of fish, and still brooding.

Something's stuck in his craw that he can't cough out. He's larger than a whale by far, but he likes whales and won't harm them. Humans… well, if he's in a foul mood (and he usually is), he'll stir the water, sending rogue waves to rock and even overturn the ships above. His greatest pleasure? Riding along tsunamis, witnessing their destructive power.

Safe to say, he doesn't like humans, and may even hate us. So why does he appear in my dreams?

Is it because I'm gay?

Yeah, I know, it's a weird leap. Hear me out.

I'm Gerry Kestrel. I'm a Strowler and a secret queer. This is how I came to be a father, and to find and lose love, all because of this bloody dragon.

I'm Gerry Kestrel. I'm a Strowler and a secret queer. This is how I came to be a father, and to find and lose love, all because of this bloody dragon.

Present

PENNY

I love the sound of applause because it means we're going to eat. Punters fill the tip jar at the edge of the stage with pounds instead of pence.

Gerry steps up to the microphone and turns up the Charm another notch, along with his Irish lilt. "You're a magnificent lot. Thank you for coming out on a Sunday afternoon. We gotta get the kids home for tea…"

"I'm starving!" My little brother, Kai, hollers from his stool while thudding his bodhrán.

"Hold on, son." Gerry's grin allows for a touch of concern in his eyes. His children need to eat.

I chew my lip as if from hunger and not from holding back my grin. I don't want to banjax my father's sham.

"With Jack's permission," Gerry looks over the heads of the audience at the pub owner behind the bar. "We'll play you one last song to pay for our supper."

The punters all turn around, giving Jack no option but yes.

"Let me check with my daughter," Da turns to me. "You have another dance in you, Penny?"

I answer with a lifted chin while taking my place center stage, hands on my hips.

"That's my girl." He turns to the rest of our band: my mother, Bridie, on fiddle and my other father, Matthew, on guitar. They nod as they finish their quick bit of tuning. He turns back to the audience with his cheeky grin. "This last song is one we fiddled around with until it suited our daughter. You might recognize it. We call it Treble Rebel."

Bridie plays the opening chords and the punters squint and frown. Recognition dawns on their faces and they clap and whistle as I dance a treble reel to our version of David Bowie's Rebel Rebel. It starts out almost identical to the original song and transforms into a more traditional reel while keeping the power hook. We save it for our finale, for a good reason. The song ends and I bow, panting, and watch pound notes get stuffed into the jar.

"Thank you," Gerry says as the applause peaks. "We are Wild Sky. We'll be back next week. In the meantime, enjoy some of the finest booze and grub in all London."

While my family packs their instruments, I go to the green room to get changed. First, I look in the mirror to see how my new costume held up. I'd finished sewing it only moments before we left for this gig. It's a simple skater-style pattern, emerald-green with Celtic knot applique, which was a bitch to stitch into stretch velvet. I spin and that's when I see it. The hem is coming out in the back.

"Pants," I mutter as I tug the dress over my head. Maybe no one noticed. Yeah, right. How embarrassing.

I change into jeans and a T-shirt and am lacing up my trainers when there's a tap on the door.

"Come in," I call out. My family file in and set down their instruments. "We're staying?"

Gerry clutches his heart. "Your doubt slays me, child."

Bridie rolls her eyes. "Charm pours from your Da like shite."

I turn to Matthew, expecting him to pile on, but he's staring at his phone, his face pinched with concern.

"What's the word?" Gerry asks him.

Matthew shakes his head. "Still not sure. Tonight, or tomorrow."

I cross all my fingers as Bridie says what I'm thinking, "I hope it's tomorrow. I want to enjoy tonight."

"You and me both, love." Gerry says with a wink. He turns to the mirror, smudging at his eyeliner, making it look as if he hasn't slept in three days.

I shake my head. His fingers are nimble enough to play almost any instrument, but he's shite with makeup. I pat the stool beside me before reaching into my purse for my cosmetic bag.

Da sits, obediently wiping away his stage makeup with the towelette I hand him. "Just a light touch, yeah? I don't want to look obvious."

I lift his chin. His blue eyes gaze up at me, trusting as a child, while I use the lash curler. "Is this what it's like to be in love?"

He grins. "I suppose."

"But you've known each other for years. My whole life."

"Years don't matter when you're in love."

I wonder if I'll feel that way, too. It seems so big and scary. I don't know that I'd like it. I apply a light coat of black mascara to his already long lashes. "Done."

Gerry examines his reflection, smiles, stands, and kisses my forehead. "Smashing. Ta, love."

"Let's go see what Charm hath wrought," Bridie says dryly.

"Finally." Kai reaches for the door handle.

As we file out to the pub, Jack motions us over to a table set with fish and chips, pints of Guinness for the adults, and lemonade for me and Kai. We voice appropriate surprise, lifting our drinks in boisterous appreciation.

After Jack walks away, proper chuffed, I lean into Gerry and whisper, "Teach me Charm."

"How old are you?"

"Fifteen, but…"

"No buts." He turns to my mother. "Bridie, did you hear the girl?"

She nods grimly. "I did, and no."

I slump back in my chair. "But I'll be sixteen in four months."

"Then you've got four months to go."

Kai shoves a handful of chips into his gob before fixing his gloat on me. I stick my tongue out at him. I might have four months, but he's got four years. He can suck that down along with those chips.

It's not fair. I know it's traditional to start Charm lessons at sixteen, but we're hardly a traditional family. We live on the Crossroads, a secret society of warriors, wanderers, beggars, and assassins. Those on the Crossroads walk the Glory Road of duty or the Wayward Way of freedom. It's obvious at a glance which way we walk, two black-haired men, one Irish, the other Chinese, a red-haired, green-eyed woman, and two brunette children, the girl with green eyes and the boy with hazel.

Bleaters, ordinary people, who wander in after the show favor us with speculative glances as they play the game of "Who Fathered Who?" They can shove it up their collective arse. Gerry and Matthew are both our fathers. Biologically, I'm Gerry's child and Kai is Matthew's, but biology doesn't mean much on the Wayward Way. The Crossroads is divided into clans. Bridie and Gerry are Strowlers, and Matthew belongs to the Two Dragon Clan. Or rather, belonged. He was kicked out, just like Bridie and Gerry were shunned, after taking up with each other, even though the domestic situation isn't what it might seem...

The pub door swings open and Gareth enters. He and Gerry exchange casual nods before he goes to the bar to order his pint. Gerry's glance lingers, though he looks away before the glow on his face becomes too obvious. Is that what love is? I mean, they saw each other yesterday.

Gareth saunters over with his pint and takes the empty seat between Gerry and Bridie. "All right."

"All right," we all reply.

He takes a chip off Gerry's plate before resting his arm behind Gerry's chair. That's the most they dare in public.

"You should've been here, Pa," says Kai. "We smashed it."

"Next time, son," he replies with a smile.

"You always say that, you bastard." Gerry tips back his pint.

"Day shows are hard for me. You know that."

Da exaggerates his sigh and his whisper as he turns to me. "Don't marry a doctor."

"Even if he's bonny?" I whisper back.

"Especially not then."

They aren't married, not yet, anyway, but close enough that we call Gareth "Pa", just like we call Gerry "Da" and Matthew "Ba." Three wonderful fathers. Makes me feel like the luckiest girl in London, despite the stares.

"How's Helena?" asks Bridie. "It's been a while since we've seen her."

"Busy," Gareth replies. "There's always a mess needs sorting when you're the chief."

"I told her that," Bridie mutters. "But did she listen?"

"You know my sister. She listened to you, she listened to me, she made up her mind and set her course."

"That's what makes her such a grand leader," says Gerry.

I lift my glass because I love Helena. "Here's to Mad Maud, Chief of the Beggar Clan."

The adults shush me, but still raise their glasses. As they drink their toast, Matthew stops mid-sip to pull out his phone. As he stares at the screen, he mirrors the intensity of his son, who's glued to a video game. I roll my eyes. Ever since our parents got Kai a phone, all he does is tap away at the screen like a little git. I'm about to say so when Ba's grim expression stops me.

Unfortunately, performing for tips and the Charmed generosity of barkeeps isn't enough to support a family of five. We all do our part. Bridie and I read palms, and Kai collects bottles and cans for recycling, but it's our fathers who make the real gelt. They're thieves of a particular kind. They retrieve stolen goods. This means anything from coercing a fence to give up his ill-gotten gain to cat burglary. They've never been caught, mainly because Matthew uses the stealth skills he learned in the Two Dragon Clan. Still, it's a dicey business. My stomach drops whenever they get a call.

"We're on," Matthew says to Gerry.

"Bugger. When?"

"Now. The client's sending round a car."

Da's grin lights up his face. Maybe it's that hit of adrenaline he craves, but this seems like something else. He looks delighted, unlike Matthew, who seems angry. He's been edgy all day, and quieter than usual, until our show broke his mood.

"Take the kids back home to the gaff, yeah?" Matthew asks Gareth.

"Sure." Gareth turns to Gerry. "We still on at Wilde's?"

Wilde's is one of the many Soho gay bars near Piccadilly Circus. I've never been, but Bridie has described it as "discreet." That sounds boring, but I guess it's not. It's where Gerry and Gareth usually meet after a show. Sometimes Bridie and Matthew join them.

Da leans into his love as close as he dares. "I'll be there at midnight, like Cinderella. Have my glass slipper ready, yeah?"

"So full of yourself."

"Would you have me any other way?"

"No."

They gaze into each other's blue eyes. Gareth has red hair and pale, freckled skin, much like Bridie. Gerry definitely has a type, but he's not bisexual. He married my mother to hide what he was. Living his truth, painful as it was, also set her free.

Bridie and Matthew kiss as Kai gags and looks away. Will my first love break my heart, too? And will I find someone to mend it? Is that how life goes?

Gerry gives me a wink. "You look after your mother and brother, now, Penny Lane."

That's my full name. Penny Lane Sparrow. It could be worse. It could be Lucy in the Sky with Diamonds Sparrow. Or would that be better? It doesn't matter. Only Gerry and Matthew call me Penny Lane, usually when they want my full attention.

My heart swells as I watch Da and Ba shrug on their leather jackets and swagger out the door. Proper wide boys they are, living for the game and the gelt that comes with it. I want to be just like them when I'm an adult. Not a thief, but I want that attitude of walking the world at my will.

We gather the instruments from the green room and leave through the pub's back entrance to the alley where our parents parked their Vespas. Usually, I ride with Matthew, Kai with Bridie, and Gerry totes the instruments strapped behind him.

Bridie takes off on her Vespa while my brother and I follow Gareth out the alley. I carry the bodhrán and Bridie's fiddle. Kai carries his guitar, and Gareth hauls Gerry and Matthew's instruments. The pub isn't far from the Beggar Abode, so I figured that's where we'd head, but we'd only gone a couple of blocks before Gareth leads us into a residential alley. The red brick apartment buildings cast long shadows across the numbered parking stalls.

"Do you have a flat here?" I ask. By "you", I mean the Beggar Clan. They have safe houses all over the city, though it'd be odd having one so close to the Abode.

Gareth grins. "No. Just got lucky."

We come to the end of the alley and find his car, a black Volvo, parked on the other side of the blue and gray rubbish bins.

"It's a proper spot, but with no number," he explains as he goes around to the back and opens the boot so we can load the instruments. "No one ever parks here except me. I think everyone thinks it's my spot."

"Cheeky," I say with admiration. Looks like Pa's a bit of a wide boy, too.

I take the front seat and Kai the back, settling next to Gareth's white coat and medical rucksack before gluing his face to his phone again.

"Was this a Bleater day?" I ask.

Gareth nods. He's what the Beggar Clan calls a plant, meaning a member planted in mundane society. When he was young, he joined the military with the agreement they'd pay his way through medical school. After becoming a doctor, he served two tours of duty before finally returning to London, his clan, and Gerry. Nowadays, he mostly serves the Beggar Clan, but remains on call in the mundane world, giving him access to medical information that could be useful to the clan.

Nameless and faceless, disregarded as human trash, the Beggars are the best source of information in the world, but they can only learn so much from sitting outside office buildings or digging through bins. Members like Gareth fill in the gaps.

Gareth presses the ignition and Bono's voice croons from the speakers. I recognize the song, Window in the Skies.

"You fancy U2?" I ask.

He doesn't reply until he's pulled out of the alley and into the street, and there's a hesitation to his tone. "I like them well enough. This song, it's kind of our song."

"Your song? You and Gerry's?"

He nods.

I blink. "But I thought your song was Oh L'Amour."

Gareth grins and shakes his head. "No. That's his song to embarrass me."

When he's in the audience, Wild Sky plays an acoustic version of the Erasure techno hit while Gerry sings directly to his love. I thought it was silly and romantic, and therefore must be their song, even though Gareth always turns bright red.

"Why Window in the Skies?" I ask.

"It was playing during a special moment in our lives." His eyes soften with his voice, as if he's reliving the memory. "Ask Gerry. It's for him to tell you."

I press my hands to my heart and sigh. "Having an 'our song' is so romantic. I wonder if anyone will ever love me like that."

His face becomes wry. "Your father and I didn't have the easiest path. Still don't. I hope yours is much easier."

"Easy doesn't mean good, Pa," Kai chimes in from the backseat. From the mouth of babes, or in this case, annoying little gits. Then he ruins it by holding out his phone and adding, "Like Mario Kart. It wouldn't be fun if it was easy."

I roll my eyes and groan.

Gareth's grin returns. "You're right, son."

But he's not. You can't compare video games to love. Can you? I mull on that for the rest of the ride home. It takes longer than usual since we're in a car and can't weave in and out of the early evening traffic. It thins out after we cross the Thames and head south, toward Clapham. The South London Caravansary Club is near the Common. Reservations are always required and never available unless you're a Sharper on the Wayward Way.

Gareth pulls up to the closed front gate. A guard steps out of the security kiosk and looks us over before asking, "Where do you walk?"

"Upon the cross," Gareth answers, making eye contact the whole time.

"Who do you serve?"

"No master but myself."

That's not true. He still walks the Glory Road, serving the Beggar Clan while being under the command of his sister, Helena, or Mad Maud as the Beggars call her. But the guard doesn't know that, and he waves us through.

We enter a wooded grove surrounded by a tall hedge hiding the barbed wire fence meant to keep out nosy Bleaters and thieving Tag Rags. Evergreen shade trees provide further privacy from the CCTV cameras on nearby buildings. Gareth steers past other pitches until we reach our gaffe in a corner stall at the far end of the park. It's our favorite spot, though we don't always get it when we come here to stay.

As we enter our caravan, Bridie is pouring herself tea. She smiles at Gareth. "Cuppa?"

He shakes his head before setting down Gerry and Matthew's guitars. "I better head back to the Abode and see if anyone needs me before I go out tonight."

She sighs. "Well, if Matty joins you at Wilde's, tell him to call me, yeah? I was up all-night fretting last time he forgot."

"Will do."

"Cheers."

"Cheers," he says as he kisses her cheek. He kisses mine as well and tousles Kai's hair before heading back out to his car.

Bridie hands me a silver tray containing a saucer of milk and a piece of bread. I go out the door and place the tray within the small circle of stones beside our stairs. Glancing around the camp, I can see other families have also placed their fairy offerings for the evening. I give a content sigh at the sense of protection this gives me.

We settled down for the evening with tea and biscuits. Bridie watches one of those baking contests on telly while Kai pokes at Pokémon or whatever on his phone. I take out my sewing machine and fix the hem on my dress. The only thing keeping it from being a perfect evening is the absence of Gerry and Matthew, but they'll be home soon enough.

If there's one thing I know about my fathers, it's that they'll never leave us.

Dream

PENNY

I walk along the edge of a cliff, ocean waves crashing wildly against the rocky shore below.

Where am I?

I glance around at the rough terrain with rolling green hills and huge, dark storm clouds brewing overhead. Ireland, but where? A faint whiff of sulfur fills the air. Kilkee, a sacred spot for Strowlers, near the lair of the great dragon Master Stoorworm. We must've parked here for the night, but I can't see our caravan anywhere. Thunder rumbles as lightning bedazzles the clouds pink, orange, and red. Its lethal beauty stirs my soul. I don't want to leave. Then a jagged bolt of lightning splits the sky and strikes the roiling surface of the ocean. The roar of thunder shakes the ground and pops my ears. Fear gets the better of me and I run. Then stop.

Gerry.

Where is he?

I turn every which way. I'm alone. No. He wouldn't leave without me. I call his name, but I'm drowned out by the rumble of thunder and a sudden wind that whips at my clothes and hair. I drop to my knees and peer over the edge of the cliff. The sea has risen to my level. I'll be swept away if I don't run, but I can't leave without him. I plunge the upper half of my body into the water to look for my father.

My gasp nearly drowns me. A huge dragon, the size of an airplane, descends into the sea. Master Stoorworm. A glowing light emanates from his chest allowing me to see his green scales and gold underbelly, and folded leathery wings. He undulates through the water, dragging a man down into his wake. Gerry! I shout my father's name, reaching out my arms. Gerry reaches back but continues to descend. Our eyes lock. Sorrow fills his face. His lips move, but I can't hear his words. All I can do is watch as he disappears into the murky depths.

Past

GERRY

"All right," says Bridie, standing above me.

"All right," I reply.

She dims her torch, scarce needed with the full moon overhead. I look up, taking in my wild girl, the wind whipping her red curls and the long shawl draped around her like a blanket. She's wearing a mere slip of a dress and her legs and feet are bare, as usual.

I pat the space beside me. She hesitates. I don't blame her. I'm sitting on the edge of a cliff, my legs dangling over the wild foam of the Irish sea. Her feet test the slippery grass before finding her perch.

A gust of wind sends ocean spray up and over us. Bridie squeals and laughs, and unlike most people, it's a lovely sound, like music. I strum my guitar again, a song I'm composing as I play. Bridie listens for a while. Then, she sings along. Not in words, but sounds that match the tune, as if we have our own secret language that is song.

Ah, she's beautiful. Green eyes, rosebud mouth, skin smooth and creamy with a sprinkle of freckles. If she were a lad, she'd be my heart's desire. My one true love. What's wrong with me? Why can't I love her like that? It'd make life so much easier.

The caravans in our Flight are parked off-road about two clicks away. A Flight is when Strowlers leave their home Nest and travel for work, either singly or in a group. It's what I've been wanting to do since I've been old enough to realize I'm different. Fly away from my family and find somewhere to belong.

Bridie shakes her head and damp, red-gold ringlets cascade over her shoulders. "Do you know where we are? Why we camped here tonight?"

I shake my head. The men talk little to me. They suspect, but they don't say.

"We're outside Kilkee, near the grove where Leannán Sidhe and Master Stoorworm coupled and conceived our people." Though it's dark, I see a blush stain her cheeks as she ducks her head. "Do you believe that?"

Believe a fairy and a dragon fucked and hid the resulting bastard amongst a wandering pack of humans? That same dragon stirs within me. Is this a waking dream? Is he here because of this place? I strum the tune to Puff, the Magic Dragon. "Sure. Why not?"

She elbows my ribs, making the tune go awry. "Strowlers have stopped here for centuries to make babies. Has no one ever told you?"

I shake my head. How do I explain the veil of contempt that's covered me in every Kestrel Nest and Flight? Everyone suspects. It's up to me to prove them wrong and I have no inclination. My family sent me to these particular Sparrows so their men could teach me to fight, and I could court their only daughter.

Every night, we'd find each other and sit like we are now. She'd cluck over the scrapes and bruises I'd gained from bare knuckle boxing with her brothers, salve and bandage me, and say funny things to make me smile. Then she'd pull out her fiddle and me my guitar, and we'd play Beatles songs or jam and make our own music. Eventually, it'll be announced that we're betrothed, whether we like it or not. I suppose I do since any other girl would be intolerable. What about her, though? She deserves a man who can be her man.

"Want to go see?" she asks?

I force a grin. "Pervert."

Her eyes go wide as if I've offended her. Then she snickers and my heart lightens. "Oisin and Sheila were the only ones who went there tonight."

My eyes widen now. "Everyone knows?"

"Well, yeah. No one wants to… you know, interrupt another couple."

Trust Strowlers to schedule sex in a sacred place. We're supposed to be virgins when we wed and then faithful spouses, but we talk about breeding as if we're livestock.

"Anyway, after they got back, I snuck out. I want to see the grove."

"You haven't before?"

She shakes her head. She doesn't say, but I can figure it out. The grove is forbidden to single people. If I go with her, it's as good as a marriage proposal. I want to run for my life, but what life do I have outside of this one? If I want to be a Strowler, a man, I have to do what all real men do. No real man would turn down an invitation like this. Either I go with her or I throw myself off this cliff. The question is, which sounds like the better deal?

She stands and holds out her hand. Her smile is playful. Hopeful. If I drop off the edge, I'll ruin her life. It's not her fault we've been thrust together. It could be so much worse. I take her hand. It's not soft and helpless. Her grip is firm and musician's callouses pad her fingertips. The feel of them stirs something in me. I leave my guitar behind and allow her to lead me like a child away from the cliff.

Using her torch, Bridie lights our way to the rough stone stairway carved into the side of the cliff. We pick our way carefully down the damp steps until we reach the beach, where I hesitate.

"What is it?" she asks.

I lift a bare foot. "I don't want to step in Oisin's spunk."

Her laughter peals like bells. No one else laughs at my jokes. Maybe that's why I've liked her from the start. She flashes the torch around the beach until it lights a spot still indented by the weight of two bodies and she leads the way toward the other end of the beach.

"The sand is still warm," I remark, surprised. The sun set hours ago.

"We're near the lair of Master Stoorworm."

I suppose that's as good an explanation as any.

We settle in the crevice between two boulders and Bridie shifts her shawl, so it covers both our shoulders. I slide my arm around her waist, and we cuddle against the damp chill of the ocean.

I don't know why it's called a grove. It's nothing more than a small beach strewn with stones and surrounded by mossy cliffs. I close my eyes, breathe in the salty air, and listen to the roar of the waves.

He's here. His long, winding reptilian body drifting through the deep. Bubbles stream from his snout. He's waiting. Urging me to action.

Oy, mate. I don't need an audience.

More bubbles stream. Then he undulates away from the coast, leaving expectation in his wake.

Like I need more pressure.

"Do you feel that?" Bridie whispers.

My eyes pop open. "Feel what?"

"I don't know. Something… mystical. As if Leannán Sidhe and Master Stoorworm were still here."

So, he's pressuring Bridie, too. Bloody bastard. My arm tightens around her. Why the hell does a dragon care if we fuck? I don't get it. Any of it. Maybe I'm dreaming. I hope so. "Yeah. I guess I feel something."

Her green eyes flash as she glances up at me. "Are you just saying that?"

Am I? I've wondered what it's like to kiss her, so I lean in. Our lips touch, press. It's nice. Of course, it is. She's nice.

Her soft gasp becomes a nervous laugh. "I guess we should go."

If I don't do this now, I never will. Bridie is my saving grace. Without her, I'll be an outcast. I swallow hard and blink back the tears filling my eyes. "I don't want to go. Do you?"

Her eyes glitter as well. Her voice trembles. "No. I want to stay here with you."

We spread her shawl on the sand and lay ourselves down. Her kisses are sweet. Her body is soft where I'd prefer it firm. We go slow since neither of us knows what we're doing. I've snogged a handful of non-Strowler lads. Hurried encounters that were little more than hand jobs. This is different. Not only because she's a girl. I have feelings for her. That she's mine and I've precious little in my life to call my own. This makes me tender and careful until… well, enough said.

I finish and it feels great. Who doesn't want to have one off? I open my eyes and Bridie is crying. Oh, Christ, I hurt her. I'm such a selfish, bloody bastard. I start rolling off her, but she reaches for my shoulders to stop me. She cups my face with tender hands and raises up for a soft kiss.

"Did I hurt you?" I whisper.

"A bit," she whispers back. "But it's supposed to hurt the first time."

Is it? That sucks. I brush a strand of hair from her cheek before kissing her forehead. "I'm sorry."

She draws me down so my head rests on her breasts. Then she strokes my hair and whispers, "Silly."

Her breasts are soft and pillowy. I wish they drove me mad with desire, but no. I enjoy the sensation, the smell of her, of us. It wasn't bad. Not at all. I can do this. I close my eyes and drift away.

Dream

GERRY

The Irish Sea is so cold. I drift closer to Master Stoorworm to feel the heat radiating off his body. Don't reptiles need heat? How does he stay warm, always coiled up and brooding?

"I possess an inner fire."

I wasn't expecting an answer, but all right, then. Good to know.

"You have conceived."

This one gets right to the point, don't he?

"First time lucky, eh?" I reply.

"Luck doesn't exist. You were meant to conceive a child upon this ground, and you did."

"Meant? Meant by who? You? You set me up?"

"You came and did as intended."

"What does that mean?" This dragon intended for me and Bridie to fuck? "Look, I don't know if you give a damn, but I'm not straight, yeah? I'm gay and you forced me to be with a girl."

"I don't give a damn, and no one forced you."

Can't argue with that or him. It's like arguing with the ocean. Still, I can't keep myself from muttering, "Life forced me."

What a weak thing to say. No wonder he doesn't respect me. A stronger man would've run away to Dublin and made his way on his wits or starved in the gutter.

"No one forced me," says Master Stoorworm. "I did what needed doing."

What is he going on about? "You mean you and Leannán Sidhe?"

The bubbles from his snout are his reply.

"No offense, mate, but according to our story, you did her and dumped her. Are you saying you needed to do that?"

More bubbles. He doesn't answer to a lowly human.

The tide carries me away. I don't resist. He's not good company. Maybe he wouldn't be so uptight if he'd gotten laid more than once.

"She wasn't my species, nor I hers, yet we lay together so you could be."

Was he talking about me or all Strowlers? Am I supposed to thank him or apologize?

"I require neither. They are coming."

"They? They who?"

I hear voices. Male voices calling our names. Bridie shakes me awake.

PENNY

I awaken with a gasp, pressing my hand to my pounding heart. A gray light creeps around the edge of the curtains. I reach for my phone to check the time. 6:23. Then I lay still and listen. A car alarm sounds in the distance. Monday morning traffic rumbles past the hedge surrounding the encampment. Within our caravan, all is as silent as it should be. I close my eyes, but I can't shake the bad feeling from the dream. Finally, I slide open the curtain enough that I can clamber down the ladder of the bunk bed I share with Kai. There's only one bedroom in the caravan, which Bridie shares with Matthew. I peer through the open door at the undisturbed bed.

My chest tightens. It's nothing. I know it's nothing because they've done this before. Stayed out all night carousing before creeping back home, drunk and apologetic. I go to the front of the van where Bridie slumps across the kitchen table, head resting in her arms, her phone beside her. Although I know better, I can't help standing on my toes and craning my neck to glimpse into the compartment above the driver and passenger seats. It's roomy enough for two, and sometimes Gerry brings Gareth home with him, but it's empty.

I sit at the table and nudge Bridie. "Mum."

She wakes with a start, flailing about before sitting up straight and asking, "They're here?"

I shake my head.

She snatches her phone and checks the screen. Her face tells me there are no messages. Air hisses between her teeth as she sets it back down. "Gareth texted me at two, saying Wilde's was closing, and the lads still hadn't shown up."

I gnaw my lip. They've done this before, too, being out on a job that took all night, unable to contact anyone. That's all this is. At least, that's what I'd think if I hadn't dreamt of Master Stoorworm.

Strowlers believe we're descended from a fairy and a dragon. The story goes that Maeve, the queen of the fairies, had a beautiful daughter, Leannán Sidhe, whose game was to seduce and abandon handsome young men. One day, she came upon a bonny lad alone on a beach. They coupled, and then he turned into the great dragon, Master Stoorworm, and dove into the sea, leaving Leannán Sidhe up the duff. Queen Maeve, pissed that her daughter got played, threatened to destroy the child, so Leannán Sidhe went in search of safe harbor. She found a traveling tinker and his wife with a newborn girl. While they slept, she exchanged her child for theirs and placed a spell on them and her daughter's descendants. Strowlers must wander forever so Queen Maeve can never find us.

It's daft as any other legend, but Strowlers believe we got our Second Sight from them, along with Charm to persuade and Fake to deceive. For whatever reason, it's considered good luck to dream of Leannán Sidhe, and bad to dream of Master Stoorworm.

I can't tell Bridie I dreamt of him. She'll lose her shit. And then five minutes later, Gerry and Matthew will walk in the door and scold me for scaring her. Not worth it.

"Why don't you have a lie down?" I say instead. "I'll start breakfast."

With a weary sigh, she lifts herself from the table before patting my cheek. "Only porridge," she says with a grumble. "They don't deserve sausage."

"What about us?"

"Hmph. Well, just enough for us, then."

I smile as she heads toward the bedroom. She knows I'll make enough for everyone. I plug in the coffeemaker and open the tin of ground beans, inhaling the heady, caffeinated scent before scooping them into the filter. I'll need a cup before I start breakfast. For some reason, I'm really sleepy. I mean, I can't keep my head up. Gripping the kitchen table, I slide onto the bench. My eyes close as my head collapses into my arms.

When I open my eyes again, my mouth is bone dry. I shake my head to clear away the remaining slumber. I blink because the light in the kitchen is completely different, as if hours had passed. Then I blink again, harder, as I realize the kitchen cupboards and drawers are all open. Who did that? Kai. Some kind of stupid joke…

A muffled shriek escapes my lips and I shrink back against the wall, glancing frantically up and down the length of our caravan. Every door and drawer hang open, but nothing has been removed, as if a storm blew through and somehow left everything undisturbed. Even the coffee maker looks as I left it, though now filled with coffee. I listen, but all I can hear is my panting breath and pounding heart.

Brave. I must be brave for my family. Make sure they're okay. I slide my feet into my slippers, exactly where I left them under the table. Then I take a deep, shaking breath before sliding off the bench. I go to the front first, and with knocking knees, climb the ladder into the cabover. The drawers hang open, but there's no sign of either Gerry or the evil bastards who did this.

I hear a muffled groan, followed by a startled cry. Kai stands outside our bunk beds, looking every which way. He jumps as he notices me, before pressing his hand to his chest. "Sis. What the hell?"

I put my finger to my lips before motioning him to follow me to the bedroom. We listen at the door. I hear only silence above our frantic breaths. Kai turns the knob and rushes inside. Our mother lays in a peaceful slumber on the bed. Same scenario with the closets and drawers. All our instruments, which had been stacked against the wall, now lay on the floor, their cases opened, but otherwise undisturbed.

A tingling sensation moves through me. This is too weird. Too deliberate. Whoever did this wanted us to see what they'd done, how we'd been at their mercy, and somehow survived.

Kai shakes Bridie until she awakens. Her confused expression, followed by her anguished shriek, drops my heart into the abyss. My stomach hurts so badly, I can barely move. She jumps out of bed and runs. Her wails echo through the caravan.

I manage to call Gareth. Words spill out and I hang up.

Whatever game Gerry and Matthew were on last night, it went horribly wrong. Bad enough that this… whatever this is… happened. Are they still alive? We are, so whoever did this might not be after blood. Maybe there's a note or message.

I search the bedroom, shaking out the rumbled bedding, searching for any clues. No notes, but maybe - I pull out my phone. No messages, but they wouldn't contact me.

I go out to the cabin, where Bridie has collapsed onto the kitchen bench. Kai sits beside her, patting her arm, his fearful face making it obvious he needs comfort, too.

We don't have time for that. "Mum, check your phone. Maybe there's a message from whoever did this."

She snatches her phone from her pocket and starts scrolling and tapping. Then it slides onto the table as she buries her shaking head in her hands.

"Mum," I say sharply. "We can't just give up."

"Don't you understand what this means? Whoever Gerry and Matty were trying to game is on the Crossroads."

I suck in a hard breath. She's right. The Crossroads forbids vengeance against children and non-combatants like Bridie. Whoever did this stretched the limits by invading our home, but leaving us unharmed preserved their honor, and honor is everything on the Crossroads.

Kai's phone rings. He yanks it from his pocket and stares at the screen. "It's Grandma."

He means Matthew's mother. I call her Auntie Enid, with her grudging permission. She wouldn't just call out of the blue. It must have something to do with her son.

Kai doesn't wait for permission to answer. "Hi, Grandma." He listens for a moment. "Yeah, they're here. I'll put the phone on speaker."

He sets his phone on the table. Bridie sucks in a tight breath before leaning forward. "Enid, hello. I'm glad you called. Um, have you heard from Matthew? He and…"

"He's gone." Auntie Enid's tone is clipped. Emotionless. It can't possibly mean the worst.

"Gone where?"

"He's dead, Bridie. Dead. Thanks to you enticing him into that life you lead. My son is dead, and it's your fault. All your fault."

Mum's face loses all expression. She stares at the phone, unblinking. Barely breathing.

I find my voice. "Auntie Enid, what do you mean he's dead? What happened?"

"What happened, Penny, is that my son met your parents, and they led him astray, off the Glory Road and onto the Wayward Way. I knew they'd be the ruin of him. I knew it."

"What do you mean? What happened?"

A male voice comes on the line. "Grandson, are you there?" It's Matthew's father, who I call Uncle Charles.

Kai's voice quavers. "Granddad, what's going on? Is my dad dead?"

"I'm sorry. Yes, he's dead."

"But… but… how? What happened?"

"We don't know. His body was left on our doorstep early this morning."

"And he was dead? I mean, right then?"

"Yes." Uncle Charles is a surgeon. If he says someone is dead, he means it.

Tears spill down Kai's cheeks. He stutters before asking, "How did he die?"

"He was shot."

A shriek escapes Bridie's lips. She snatches the phone. "I want to see him. We'll be right over."

"You will do no such thing," snaps Auntie Enid. "Whoever killed him knows who he is, who we are. I won't have you here, bringing any further danger to us." She takes a crisp breath. "Besides, Matthew isn't here. We called the *kongsi*, and our clan chief graciously offered to take care of his body. There won't be a proper funeral, thanks to you and that Gerry, but…"

"Gerry," I gasp. "What happened to him?"

"How should we know? He wasn't with Matthew, if that's what you mean. Now, Charles and I are on our way to your trailer park. You'll give us Kai, and we'll take care of him from now on."

"What are you on about?" whispers Bridie.

"You ruined our son. We won't let you ruin our grandson."

Bridie jabs the screen, ending the call.

We collapse into each other, sobbing. Even as my tears fall, I can't believe it's real. I don't want to! It must be some cruel hoax, some way for Enid and Charles to keep Matthew from us. But Matthew wouldn't let them, not if he was alive. He'd be here, right now, comforting us. No. No! How can he be dead? And what about Gerry?

Someone pounds on the front door.

We flinch. Then freeze. Is it Enid and Charles, come to snatch Kai away? No, they wouldn't be allowed into the park. It must be Gerry! But why would he knock? Maybe he lost his keys while fleeing whoever killed Matthew. I jump up and throw myself at the door, flinging it open.

It's Gareth. Without Gerry.

At the foot of the stairs, I see the silver tray I set the night before. The saucer's cracked and the stones scattered as if kicked aside by a careless foot. Has Leannán Sidhe forsaken us? Why?

Fresh tears spill down my cheeks. I can't believe it. I won't. He must be alive. I can feel it.

But where is he?

Dream

PENNY

I dive off the edge of the cliff, into the murky depths of the Irish Sea. The vortex sucks me into the warm water, heated by the wake of the dragon spiriting away my father. I swim after them, going deeper and deeper, knowing my lungs won't last, but unwilling to stop.

I can't stop. I must rescue my father, even if it kills me.

"Penny, no." Gerry's voice, gentle in my ear, as if he's beside me.

I redouble my effort, arms burning, chest bursting, until I have no more breath. That doesn't matter. I can do this without breath.

I keep going, reaching out to my father. He shakes his head, eyes aching, as he reaches back.

Our fingers almost

almost

almost

touch.

Master Stoorworm swishes his tail.

A wave hits me like a roller coaster, hurling me in the opposite direction, Gerry disappearing into the bubbles churning after me. My body turns somersaults as I try fighting it until I break the surface of the water. Oxygen sears my depleted lungs. I gasp and paddle like a drowning dog. Then another wave lifts me up and hurls me onto the shore.

Sand coats my body, the grains lacerating my raw skin. I raise myself to my knees, stare out at the remorseless sea, and weep.

GERRY

"Hurry, hurry," Bridie whispers as she tugs her dress over her head.

I've got my trousers zipped and I yank on my T-shirt before standing.

"Bridie! Gerry!" The voices are closer, echoing off the cliffs.

I reach down and help her to her feet. She grabs her shawl on the way up. We flee toward the boulders, but torches are already shining down on us.

"Freeze, the both of you!"

We freeze because what else can we do?

Bridie's face is pale as the moon set with twin emeralds. Her mouth is a slash of fear. Her hand squeezes mine tight. She licks her lips. "Don't say a word. Let me do the talking."

I wasn't planning on talking. What is there to say?

The men come barreling toward us. Bridie's brothers, cousins, and uncles, all itching to thrash me within an inch of my life, but I've proved I'm a man, so it's worth it, yeah?

We're yanked apart, our hands reaching for each other as we're dragged away. I'm thinking of myself. What will they do to her, the daughter who disgraced them?

"Don't hurt her," I call out.

"Shut yer gob, ye little shite," snaps Oisin, her oldest brother. He's a professional boxer and I know he can't wait to use me as his punching bag.

"Oisin, please," Bridie cries out.

"Not a word from you, girl. Not from either of you. Come along."

The hands that drag me along aren't as rough as expected. No one smacks me upside the head or even threatens my life and limb. They even stop so I can retrieve my guitar. When we reach the encampment, they thrust Bridie into her Uncle Kevin's caravan. She cries out my name as the door slams on her. I want to fight back and grab her so we can run away... where? Between us, we have nothing. We'd be outcast and wasn't that the whole point? To sleep with her so I can belong.

I'm released and allowed to slink into Oisin's caravan, where I've been staying during this Flight. In the pit of my stomach, I feel the sharp pang of all my yearning to find somewhere to belong. Now, I realize it's not here, but it's too late.

Oisin's wife, Sheila, is standing, arms folded at the kitchen counter. They have no children yet, while Christy, Oisin's younger brother, already has three. Hence their frolic in the grove, I suppose. Did Master Stoorworm come to Oisin in a dream and tell him he hit fertile soil? My stomach drops further at the thought. I don't want Bridie to be pregnant. I should've thrown myself off that cliff when I had a chance.

Sheila heaves a long sigh before nodding for me to sit at the kitchen table. She pours two cups of tea before joining me.

"Ta," I mumble as she sets a cup before me. I take a sip and feel some relief as the hot liquid takes the edge off my shivers.

She leans back in her chair and stares at me for a long moment. "Did you have your way with her?"

I manage not to sputter. More like Bridie had her way with me, but I don't say that. I could've said no, and I didn't. I made her believe I wanted her as much as she wanted me. That makes me a little piece of shite who deserves what's coming to him.

Maybe this is a good thing. Maybe, after beating the living shite out of me, they'll send me packing and I can return to the Kestrel Nest, shamed but proven a man. But what if that damn dragon is right? What if there is a baby? What kind of man would leave Bridie to face the consequences alone?

"Do you love her?" asks Sheila.

"More than anyone." My voice trembles because it's true. No one has ever been as kind to me as Bridie or treated me like I'm brilliant and fun.

Sheila's face softens. She rises without a word and leaves the caravan. I hurry to the bathroom. I want a shower in the worst way. Wash off the evidence? Or maybe I prefer to be clean when Bridie's brothers take turns pummeling me.

When I get out, Oisin has taken my place at the table with his wife, and a cup of tea. They stop talking, their sharp eyes tracking me as if I'm the sparrow and they're the kestrels, waiting for a show of weakness. I climb the ladder into the bunk at the front of the cab and slide the curtain closed. I pull the blankets to and fro, as if settling down, before leaning as close as I dare to the edge of the curtain.

"What else should we have expected?" whispers Sheila. "Everyone says she's touched by Leannán Sidhe, the way she wanders about by herself, singing and dancing. Your family should've found a firm man, not a pretty boy who loves music. Of course, they fell from grace. How could they not?"

"My folks have always been too soft on her," grumbles Oisin. "The only girl and all that. They wanted a compatible lad and settled on him. Like as not, they're both to blame. Time's come. We've waited too long."

My heart lurches as Oisin rises and I freeze, expecting him to yank me from my bed. Instead, I hear the door open and them exit the caravan. I exhale and lay back down on the mattress. He must be gathering his brothers. All I can do is lie here and wait until I'm pulled out to face my sentence. I stare at the ceiling, flinching at every sound, until my lids droop and I drift off.

I awaken to the familiar sense of motion. I look out the window, watching as we pass rolling green hills dotted with sheep. The caravan has taken Flight. Maybe that's why they delayed my punishment. I slide open the curtain and cautiously climb down the ladder. Oisin ignores me, his eyes on the road as he drives. Sheila glances at me from the passenger seat.

I clear my throat. "G'morning."

She nods.

I grab my clothes and head for the bathroom. When I come back out, there's a mug of coffee and a bowl of oatmeal waiting for me on the table. I'm not hungry, but I tuck in, determined to eat and drink every drop lest I offend. After a few minutes, I summon the courage to ask, "Where we headed?"

"The Sparrow Nest," Sheila replies.

I draw my breath. So, I'm to face the judgment of Bridie's parents. That makes sense since they rule that roost. Bridie's mother being the Mother Bird and her father being the Upright Man. Rather than travel, they stay put, keeping the Nest a haven for Strowlers and a home base for their Sparrow kin. I grimace because I can't think of a worse life. All I want is my own caravan, so I can hit the road. I can't do that without a wife. Too bad I mucked up this chance.

I miss Bridie. I miss our chemistry, jamming together on these long rides, learning new songs from each other, or making up our own. Cozying up with cups of tea while trading gossip outside the earshot of Oisin and Sheila.

My throat tightens. That's the worst part of this. I'm losing my only friend. Why couldn't I have been stronger? How does having sex with a woman prove I'm a man, anyway? It just proves I'm an idiot.

The Sparrow Nest is located outside Bray, a small town south of Dublin. After we pull into the compound and park, I watch out the window as Christy and his wife lead Bridie into her parents' house. She looks over her shoulder and sees me. Her eyes sparkle like green emeralds. Tears spill down her cheeks. I can't let her face this alone. I rush to the door, but Oisin blocks my way. Taking me by the scruff of the neck, he hauls me out of the way before opening the door and heading out.

Sheila crosses her arms and shakes her head. "You'll only do more harm than good, ya eejit."

"But Bridie… it's not her fault. None of this is her fault." It's the dragon's fault, but I don't add that.

"You're an upright lad, I'll give you that. No one will hurt the girl. Arrangements are being made. You want my advice, you sit tight, keep your head down, and everything will work out as it should."

What can I do but take that advice?

A week passes in a strangely normal manner. I'm tasked with what earns my keep. I've a knack for repairing and refurbishing scooters. Once my family discovered this skill, they kept me busy, as have the Sparrows, without my reaping any benefit aside from grudging nods for work well done. In the evenings, I spar with Bridie's brothers, none of them hitting me any harder than usual. I know better than to think I've escaped punishment, if that's what you want to call it.

Every day, I watch as Bridie is driven away with her sisters-in-law and mother. They return with a multitude of packages, which are loaded into a caravan big enough for a small family starting out on their own.

Which is to say, though no one's said a word, I'm not surprised to find a tuxedo waiting for me when I wake up Saturday morning. Sheila had taken my measurements a few days ago. She didn't have to speak. I knew.

I shower and shave, though I'm shaking so badly, it's a wonder I don't slit my throat. Maybe I should. That would end this fucking misery. I stare at myself in the mirror. Black, curly hair, blue eyes, pale skin. I want to find my heart's desire and be his. If I can't have that, what's the point? I stare at the razor in my shaver. Ah, Bridie. What would happen to her if I killed myself rather than marry her? What if she is carrying my wain? She'll never be my heart's desire, but she makes me happy, and I can do everything in my power to make a good life for her and our child. Maybe that's enough.

I put down the blade and put on my suit like a good boy. I even choke down the porridge Sheila gives me because I know what's coming. Oisin pours a shot of whisky into my coffee. I drink it down like mother's milk.

He slaps my back. "Good lad. We're off."

I don't ask where. I get into a limousine, scrunched between Oisin and Christy. Bridie's parents sit across from us and eyeball me like I'm a thief in the night. Yet there's something in their eyes, in the twitch of their mouths, that tells me they're well-pleased. They've trapped someone to take their fey daughter off their hands. If that's the case, then I'm glad it's me. They don't deserve her.

We're driven to one of those wee churches that Strowlers count on for sacraments without a lot of questions. After we climb out, Christy hands me a flask. I take a sip, allowing the whiskey burn to clear my head and soothe my nerves. I hold it out and he shakes his head.

"Keep it. You'll need it."

He's got that right.

We enter the church and I go straight to the men's room, into a stall, and puke up the entire contents of my stomach. Then I wash my face, take a swig from Christy's flask, and head back out to face the rest of my life.

Flanked by Oisin and Christy, I head up the church aisle, the eyes of the packed pews boring into me. Strowler weddings have no invitation. Anyone in the area is welcome and everyone shows up.

I don't care about that.

My eyes are on the front of the church and the man standing to the right of the priest.

My oldest brother. Oren. The man who dedicated his life to beating the pansy out of me, the one who made leaving our Nest to live with the Sparrows seem like the only way out.

My chief tormentor is my best man?

No. Fucking. Way.

As if I had a choice.

I come up beside him and enjoy my only triumph over him. My height. I'm tall and lanky like my mam's kin. Oren takes after Da, with short legs, long arms, and ginger brown hair he keeps buzzed and bearded. He makes up for lack of inches with bulging muscles and fists that pack a mean punch. His hazel eyes favor me with his typical stone-dead stare.

We don't speak.

Mammy tries smiling at me from the front pew, her blue eyes a storm of worry. Da died a few years ago, freeing her and me from his violent temper and presence here today. My siblings give the usual scowls reserved for me, the youngest, the family whipping boy. They doubtless had to pay a dividend for my taking Bridie's prenuptial cherry.

Looking at them makes me feel better about everything. They've offloaded me for good, which means I'm done with them. I take some comfort and courage in that.

Bridie's family sits across the aisle. Their expressions are neutral. They're offloading a trouble child, too, but no hard feelings. So long as I do well by their daughter, I'm welcome among them.

My stomach churns again, and I long for a swig from Christy's flask. Sweat pools in my armpits and coats my brow. My chest rises and falls too quickly. I need to get out of here.

Now!

My mouth opens, ready to plead the need for the loo.

Too late.

The organ strikes up the wedding march. The door to the sanctuary swings open and in she walks on her father's arm.

Bridie.

I gasp because she's beautiful. A crown tops her head, matching the diamonds at her neck and wrists. Her long red hair lays loose on her bare shoulders when others would've worn it up. Instead of drowning in a sea of lace, she's sleek in satin, showing just how curvaceous and desirable she'd be to the right man.

I smile, glad that she chose a gown that suits her rather than the conventions of the usual Strowler bride. Maybe that's why I love her. And make no mistake, I do love her. I just wish my body could react the way my heart does.

I can feel Oren eyeballing me, keen for any hint of reluctance or revulsion. I ignore him and concentrate on the love I feel for her, my savior, the girl who will free me from him.

As she reaches the altar, her eyes look at me pleadingly, communicating what I already know. This wasn't her doing. She didn't mean to trap me, anymore than I meant to trap her, yet here we are.

As she lets go of her father, I reach out my hand. She takes hold of me, white knuckled, as if reaching for a lifeline.

The ceremony blurs by. My stomach doesn't act up again until I hear those fatal words:

"I now pronounce you man and wife."

I'm married. My own man. Who'll never love another man. That's the price of this freedom.

Bridie and I don't have a chance to talk until the reception, when we're alone, in front of everyone, for our first dance. The room darkens and Bridie flinches as the spotlight hits us. I take her in my arms and feel some of her tension ease as we sway to My Heart Will Go On.

Not my first choice. What would I have chosen? Maybe Tainted Love by Soft Cell.

"I'm sorry," she whispers as she rests her cheek on my shoulder.

"Don't be," I whisper back. "We were going to be married eventually, whether we liked it or no."

"And you don't?"

"No. I do. If I was going to marry any girl in this world, Bridie, it'd be you."

She raises her head, her eyes brimming with my words, spoken with the utmost sincerity. Really, I'm lucky. It could be so much worse.

Celine finishes wailing on about love and we're parted again. She to be fussed over by the womenfolk and me to drink with the lads.

Before I can join them, Oren reaches up to wrap his hand around my neck, his calloused fingers digging into my flesh.

"I need to school the lad for a moment," he says with a wink and a smirk before hauling me outside.

It's dark and cloudy, threatening to rain like it has all day. The lights of the parking lot beam down harshly on his face as he lets go of me and wipes his hand on his trousers. Then he wastes the effort by jabbing my chest.

"Maybe you've shammed that girl and her kin, but you haven't shammed me. I know what you are. I promised Mammy I'd give you a chance, so here it is. Stay out of Ulster. Don't cross the border. Not for any reason." He leans in close. Too close. I force myself not to recoil at the stench of his breath and sweat. "If I hear that you've played the Sodomite and disgraced us, I'll kill you."

He shoves me against the wall and strides inside.

I exhale and take out the flask - my flask, now, I guess, and raise it in a toast. Stay out of Ulster? My fucking pleasure.

The door swings open, and I brace myself for round two, but

it's Bridie. She leans beside me and holds out her hand for the flask. I hand it to her.

"What was that all about?" she asks before taking a swig.

"Oren was letting me know how much he despises me."

"That wee shite? Don't pay him any mind."

So much she doesn't know.

Rain falls. We huddle under the awning, passing the flask back and forth, and everything feels so much better.

"How do you feel about going to London?" I blurt out.

Her eyes widen with her gasp. I expect her to say no. New Strowler brides don't venture far from home the first year of marriage.

"Really?" she asks, breathless.

I nod.

She squeals before hugging me. "When do we leave?"

I exhale. I really am lucky. And maybe in London I can find my way to loving her like she deserves to be loved.

Dream

GERRY

During the three-hour ferry ride from Dublin to Holyhead, Bridie, in full honeymoon bloom, wants to spend the time knocking boots. I beg off, pleading seasickness while clutching my stomach with a moan.

Her eyes narrow. This is the third time I've denied her rights to my body. Well, second and a half. On our wedding night, we were both too busy puking from all the booze poured down our throats. The next night, I begged off, pleading the devil of a hangover. Today, seasickness. Tomorrow…

Is tomorrow. Maybe I can face it all better once we're in London.

Bridie settles beside me. We scoot about until she's wrapped in my arms and her sigh becomes content, for now.

I want to want her. I don't want to be her sham husband, like Oren accused me. Breathing in her scent, sweet and sharp, like vanilla and orange, I long for something muskier. Funny thing is, in terms of looks, she suits me well. I'd love a lad with red hair, eyes of green or blue, pale, freckled skin, a spare, muscular frame, and a face with full lips and cheekbones sharp enough to cut my flesh… I picture him, my heart's desire, and something stirs within me.

Then I breathe in my wife again and squeeze my heart dry against such thoughts. It doesn't help. I need to relax. Close my eyes. Seasickness was a sham. I've always liked ferry rides. The roll of the waves relaxes me, lulling me into a slumber.

As I drift off, I sense Master Stoorworm's presence. He's swimming beneath our ship, hastening the tide to draw us toward Wales.

"What's the damn hurry?" I ask him.

He doesn't reply.

I must be dreaming. Why would that daft dragon care if I were heading for London? I huff out my irritation and deepen my slumber.

In London, it's cold and dark, with the rain blowing sideways in sheets. Bridie, dressed in rags, huddles in a doorway, the awning offering minimal protection from the weather. She cradles a precious bundle, rocking back and forth, shivering as she sings.

> "Oh, once a young man learned to love me,
> And he taught me to do the same.
> And now, oh now, he's gone and left me.
> And on my brow, there's written shame.
> See how my sisters they despise me,
> And my brothers do the same.
> And my father says he will not own me,
> And my mother hangs her head in shame.

Although my clothes are going ragged,
Still, they'll keep my baby warm.
Sleep on, sleep on my green-eyed treasure,
Oh, our wandering days will soon be done.
See how those London Lights are shining
Through the frost and falling snow.
Sleep on, sleep on my green-eyed treasure,
Oh, your mother's got nowhere to go."

I wake with a start, my heart pounding. Then I realize Bridie still lies in my arms and I breathe a little easier. My arms tighten around her, and I kiss her cheek. She stirs, her lips forming a smile, but she doesn't awaken.

I swear, on whatever I hold holy… that dragon, I guess… that I'll never abandon her and our child. No matter what or who may come.

Present

PENNY

My dream jolts me awake. Something to do with Gerry and the dragon, and… something. I grasp at the dissolving threads of the dream. Pearls. There were pearls and…

Nothing. I can't remember.

Closing my eyes, I relax into the familiarity of the top bunk bed. Then I hear the whoosh of a train passing through a nearby tunnel, and I know I'm far from home.

With a sigh, I pull aside the curtain and climb down the ladder. We're not in our caravan. We threw ourselves upon the mercy of the Beggar Chief and she, in her mercy and love for us, offered us refuge in her Abode. By all rights, we should've gone first to the London's Strowler Nest. Thing is, the Upright Man who rules that roost is a bellend who doesn't accept Strowlers on the Wayward Way. Our other option is to go to the Sparrow Nest whence Bridie first flew. Technically, they could reject Bridie as a fallen woman, a trollop who lived with two men, except she begat two children and they can't, with honor, reject us.

We don't go that route because Bridie isn't capable of getting out of bed, let alone pleading her way back into the life she rejected. And that's a good thing because I don't want to leave London. I won't. I'm not going anywhere until we find Gerry.

I poke my head into the bedroom, where my mother remains collapsed upon her grief, wound in tear-soaked sheets. My nose wrinkles at the sour scent of alcohol. I creep in and lift a half-empty whiskey bottle off the floor. Bridie's normally vibrant red hair lies dull and greasy on her pasty skin. I've yet to tell her of my dreams of Master Stoorworm. How can I, with the state of her? Maybe I never will.

I take the whiskey bottle to the kitchenette and pour the rest down the drain. Then I crack open the curtain above the sink and peer out the window. Beggars walk along the platform, talking and laughing, their lives not ruined by death.

A poster on the wall reads in bold red letters: WARNING LIVE TRACK. The track hasn't been live since the 1950s when the station was abandoned, and the decommissioned trains left on the tracks. Then the Beggars bought the station, making it their Abode, and turning the trains into living quarters. We're stowed in the guest car at the end of the track, safe from everything but fear and misery.

I go to the bathroom to wash my face and get dressed, just because it's something to do. As I step out, the bottom bunk curtain twitches open and Kai rolls out of bed, clutching his phone. I can tell from the dark smudges under his eyes he's spent another night burying his grief in the depths of a game.

"All right," I say.

He shakes his head and brushes past me into the loo.

Nothing's all right, or ever will be again, not with Matthew dead and Gerry missing. I haven't teased him once for playing games. I've spent hours watching videos to numb the pain, and I'm sick of it. Sick of being in this box surrounded by the rattle and hum of passing trains. I need to be outside, turning London upside down and inside out until I find my father. Tears fill my eyes. I slide open the door and step out to keep myself from crying.

I wander down the platform, its round, overhanging lamps providing a warmer light than a typical underground station, and run my fingers along the green and white tiles, tracing the mosaic patterns and phrases on the walls: TO THE STAIRS, NO EXIT, GRAY CLOAK STATION. When I was a child, I loved coming down here and studying the faded adverts for Spam and Ovaltine, and posters for I Was a Teenage Werewolf and Les Girls. I pestered Gerry about wanting to see those movies, but he brushed me off, until my tenth birthday, when he surprised me with both and our family had a popcorn party…

A hard lump forms in my throat. I swallow to loosen it and focus instead on the Beggar family walking toward me. A husband and wife, and two kids, a boy and a girl, all dressed in rags, on their way above ground to plead poverty to the Mundanes. That's what the Beggar Clan calls ordinary, non-Crossroads people. Strowlers call them Bleaters. Both our clans make money off them, though the Beggars argue that they're more honest in their dealings.

I snort. As if. The Beggars not only pretend to be destitute and take whatever cash people give, they also spy on designated marks and sell that information for top dollar. Strowlers use

Charm to entice Bleaters to have their fortunes read, or take a chance at a rigged shell game, or pay dearly for manual labor they might not actually need. Ethically, we're not so different. Sure, the Beggars use their funds to help the Mundane poor, but that's their Glory Road. Each clan is different.

For Strowlers, our Glory Road is traveling and living off our wits and hard labor. That means the men work odd jobs and take on bare knuckle boxing bouts. The women marry young, have children, keep the caravan clean, and tell fortunes to earn extra gelt.

That life wasn't for Bridie and Gerry. They were musicians and wanted to perform, not conform. So, off they popped to London to walk the Wayward Way. Matthew soon joined them, and everyone believed Bridie had two husbands. She let them believe it to protect Gerry. Being gay is the worst crime among agro Glory Road types. Worse than a Devil's Triangle, what they call a woman with two men, so long as the blokes aren't getting it on, and Gerry and Matthew made it clear they weren't.

Still, Gerry's agro family shunned him, claiming he dishonored them, and honor is everything on the Crossroads. Could they have something to do with his disappearance? Have they found out about him and Gareth? Because if they have…

My stomach drops as I reach the other end of the platform and stop. I could continue into the tunnel, walking along the narrow ramp until I find my way out of the underground and to the streets of London where I can search for Gerry.

Or get hopelessly lost in the maze of interconnecting passages and hope that whoever finds me is a member of the Beggar Clan and not some desperate tag rag who found their way underground. If… when I go searching for Gerry, it will be a planned endeavor and not on the whim of desperate emotion.

I turn and head back down the platform, passing more Beggars, dressed in curated rags, on their way to earn their gelt. Safe within their Abode, they chat and smile, saving their doldrums for the Mundane world. How can they sleep in these musty trains with the constant whoosh and rumble from the adjacent tunnels? Don't they long for fresh air and sun and stars? Maybe it helps they don't have grief heavy on their chests and fear constantly stirring their minds.

I reach our car and am about to go inside when I hear the familiar tap of a cane and my heart lifts ever so slightly. The Beggars on the platform move aside and nod as their chief, the Beggar Queen, Mad Maud, walks past them, heading for me.

She's dressed in rags, the same as them, and yet shines like a diamond amongst them, flash in her thick-soled boots, striped socks, and multilayered distressed plaid dress crimped at her waist with a wide brown belt, its excess length tucked over and dangling down her leg. Red-gold hair piles haphazardly atop her head, held in place with a variety of clips and bows. Her right-hand curls around the silver handle of the staff that represents her authority as the Beggar Chief.

Ordinarily, I'd give a cheeky grin before running up to her and commenting on her style, which I adore. All my life, I've aspired to be her, bold, brave, daring. Now, I stand rooted in place, fearful of whatever news she might bring.

She holds a scrap of paper out to me. "I have a number."

I don't take it. Instead, I open the door and stand aside to let her in and away from the prying eyes of her clan.

"Auntie Helena!" Kai jumps up from a bench and into her embrace.

She kisses his forehead and rubs his back. I know she'd do the same for me, but I can't hug her. Not with that piece of paper between us.

She glances around, sees the empty fifth of whiskey on the counter, and sighs, perhaps weary of being the strong one for us while also leading her clan. "Where's your mother?"

"In bed," I reply.

"I'll get her. Make coffee. Gareth will be here soon." She heads for the other end of the car.

While I set up the coffeemaker, Kai, unprompted, starts making toast. I mouth the words, thank you, and he nods, his eyes worried. Neither of us have seen Bridie eat since we got here.

There's a tap on the side of the car, and I slide open the door to let Gareth in. His cheeks are hollow and his eyes smudged dark, as if he's eaten and slept as little as us. We embrace and he holds me tight, a piece of Gerry not swallowed by the ground.

"Who's number is it?" I ask.

He holds me at arm's length. "Gerry's mother."

I close my eyes as I exhale. "All right. As long as it's not him."

Gareth doesn't ask who I mean. He knows.

Oren Kestrel. Gerry's oldest brother. The one person we know wants Gerry dead.

Then I remember my dream from last night.

Dream

PENNY

Gerry rests upon a bed of pearls in a cavern glistening with gold and sharp with rubies, emeralds, sapphires, and diamonds. The air is opalescent, thick, and shimmering. It hurts to breathe. The pressure of the ocean bears down, threatening to crush me.

My father's body seems to glow with life, though he's motionless, breathless, pulseless. I turn to the dragon curled atop his hoard, tail wrapped around him like a cat, his bearded chin resting atop a rusty anchor that sank with its ship centuries ago.

"He's dead?" I ask.

Master Stoorworm is silent, watching me like a cat, wondering when best to pounce.

"Do you know who killed him? Was it Oren?"

The dragon blinks, a scaly lid falling over each glowing red eye. Was that yes or no? Or just a blink? His massive sides expand and contract, as if heaving a sigh. He shifts a little, gold coins and precious jewels rolling off his mound. Then he opens his mouth wide.

This is it. He's going to torch me for trespassing. My eyes squeeze shut as I brace myself. Heat radiates on my skin as the sulfur stench of his breath reaches me first. Then…

Nothing.

I open my eyes as his heavy head slides off the anchor and onto his front claws.

He's asleep.

What the hell?

Wait. This is good. While he's sleeping, I can spirit away my father's body. I try taking a step forward and find myself frozen in place. I can still use my voice.

"Why did you bring me here? What do you want?"

But the dragon didn't bring me here. Gerry did. He's trying to tell me something. What?

I want to shake him, make him wake up and come home, or at least speak.

"Da, what is it? Why am I here? What happened to you?"

Treasure.

The word blows across my skin as if by a breeze.

Is Gerry the treasure? Or did whoever kill him see him as a treasure? That rules out Oren. He saw his brother as trash, with no value. But why would someone kill Gerry if they valued him?

Or was treasure the death of him?

What was he and Matthew trying to steal?

Past

GERRY

I don't ask for trouble. Really, I don't, but it's like I've got a bloody bell around my neck.

For example, I don't force Bleaters to play a shell game. I'm amazed at how many of them do. They've got to know it's a trick, yeah? Sleight of hand, slipping the pea out of the shell, into your palm, and under another shell. Mind you, Strowlers are better at it than most, and I'm better at it than most Strowlers. I use Charm to lure the Bleaters in and channel the magic into my hands, making them deft beyond the reckoning of the human eye. Or phone, which is how I got into this mess.

While I'm working my gull, collecting his gelt, some bright boy in the crowd that surrounds us whips out his phone and films me. This happens all the time and I'm not worried. I just stop working my game and play straight. There's a two-in-three chance I'll win, and I do. I try not looking too smug as I shove his pounds in my pocket.

"The pikey's cheating you, mate," brays Bright Boy. He holds out his phone for Gull's scrutiny. I don't run or protest because I know I didn't cheat. He jabs a finger at the screen. "See, right there, right there."

I keep my voice calm and friendly, inviting the gull to take my side. "There's nothing to see because I didn't cheat. Go on and film another round. You'll see." I set up the shells as I speak.

Gull wavers between me and the screen. He knows there's no proof. He wants to believe me.

"You gonna let that gyppo rob you blind?" asks Bright Boy.

I need to Charm him, too, but this is where it gets complicated. Gull was open to my initial persuasion, but not Bright Boy. While I try to sense an opening, my hold on Gull collapses.

Bollocks.

Gull's eyes narrow in a hard glare. "Gimme back my money."

I shake my head. "I won fair and square, mate."

"You cheating piece of shit."

"Show me where I cheated." I turn to Bright Boy. "Show me."

Bright Boy holds his phone close. "No way. You'll grab it and run off or steal my information and sell it on the dark web."

I know what's happening. The video doesn't show shite. Bright Boy's giving his fellow Bleater a chance to get back his money.

Gull jabs my chest. "Money. Now, or I'll call the cops."

I call his bluff, because the *gardai* don't care about shell games. "Fine. I'll wait."

His face reddens. Flecks of spittle fly from his mouth as he shouts, "Give me my money, you filthy gyppo."

He's baiting me, daring me to react and give him an excuse to call the *gardai*. Much as I want to punch him in the face, I ignore him, shoving the shells and pea into my pockets, and folding my table. I try pushing through the crowd, but they back me up against the wall.

"Give him back his money."

"Cheater."

"Pikey."

"Thief."

Gull grabs hold of my table and yanks. I yank it back. He doubles up his fist. The crowd howls. I hold up the table like a shield. If I break it over his ugly pate, I'll go to jail. I think of Bridie waiting in our caravan, heavy with our child. London Lights starts playing in my mind. It's a hell of an earworm.

"Oi!" a man shouts as he shoulders his way through the crowd. And, Lord, what a man. Tall, red hair, broad shoulders, blue eyes, and cheekbones that can cut diamonds. He looks a couple of years older than me, dressed like a typical London lad in jeans, a T-shirt, and a black leather jacket. Our eyes meet and my heart pounds even harder. If he's an undercover copper, I'll go willingly.

He stands between me and Gull and spreads his arms wide. "He's not a cheat. I won a tenner off him yesterday. So, move on, yeah? If he beat you, he won fair and square."

"You with him?" demands Gull.

"No. Like I said, I played yesterday and won. I won't stand by and let you accuse an innocent man."

Over his shoulder, I widen my eyes so I'm the picture of outraged innocence, though I'm wise enough not to speak.

"Just because you won yesterday doesn't mean he didn't cheat me today," Gull exclaims, but he's lost his momentum. The crowd disperses and even Bright Boy slinks away. Gull huffs, shakes his fist at both of us, and stalks down the street, profanity-laced rage trailing behind him.

I lean against the wall and exhale, my knees still shaking. "Thanks, mate, but I don't recall you winning a tenner off me."

The man smiles. He has white teeth and freckles. I don't know how my knees are holding me up. Then he says, "Walk in peace."

I blink. He's a Sharper, one who walks on the Crossroads, but not a Strowler. "Walk in peace," I say cautiously. "What clan?"

"I'm a Beggar."

"Get out," I scoff. No way he belongs to the Beggar Clan. He's too clean, and that scarf wound round his neck looks to be from some posh university.

"I am. I'm a plant, someone planted in the Mundane world, so I can run interference, like I just did for you."

I nod. "Clever." And not surprising. The Beggar Clan is the first and oldest clan on the Crossroads, and the London clan has been in operation since, well, since there's been a London. I want to keep him talking, but my Charm has deserted me. I search for words, but all I can do is hold out my hand. "Gerry Kestrel."

His firm grip makes my knees go weak again. I want to fall into him, but I manage to keep my balance. I watch his lips repeat my surname. "Kestrel, eh? Well, I figured you for a Strowler. I'm Gareth Abram."

He lets go, and my hand feels the lack of him. I press my palm against my thigh to keep his heat. Somehow, I say, "Fancy a drink?"

His mouth opens, and he sucks in a breath before breathing out, "Sure. Mumpers?"

Now I hesitate, trying to look casual. Mumpers Hall is an all-haven, a Crossroads pub where anyone of any clan or walk is welcome. No fighting allowed. But if we go in there, it could get back to Oren that I was having a drink with a man I'd just met. He'd think the worst. I don't want that pressure. I want to go someplace where I can moon over this lad in peace.

"There's an Irish pub around the corner. The Star and Plough. It's where I go to have a piss or hide if things…" How do I explain my inept mishandling of those damn Bleaters?

"Get dodgy?"

"Yeah."

"It happens."

To me? All the time, but it never comes with a side order of tall, ginger, and handsome, and I'm going to make the most of that.

The Star and Plough is literally around the corner, in a building painted yellow and green, and the usual sign promising Guinness is served. The dark wood interior is more subdued, with narrow windows, red carpeted floor, shabby but sturdy tables and chairs, and an equally shabby but sturdy stage where Bridie and I will perform this Friday night…

Shite.

I try not to panic as the owner, Shane, glances up at me and calls out, "All right, Gerry."

"All right," I reply and quickly add, "Can I get a Guinness for me and him?" I turn to Gareth. "Guinness all right with you, mate?"

He smiles, little crinkles appearing in the corners of his eyes, and my heart pounds. "Guinness is fine."

As Shane pulls our pints, I pray he doesn't ask about Bridie. Fortunately, his eyes are glued to the football game on the screen on the opposite wall. I pay with Gull's money and lead Gareth to the quieter end of the bar, away from Shane and the punters who are watching the game with him.

We settle in a booth in the Irish kitsch corner, its walls hung with stain glass shamrocks and photos of Irish poets. Gareth glances at the one next to his head. "You fancy Yeats?"

I know who Yeats is, but I can't say I fancy him because, truth is, I can barely read. Just enough to make out road signs, menus, and the like. I've never read a book or a poem in my life. Both Bridie and I memorize the lyrics we sing from the songs we love. I don't want him to know what an eejit I am, so I just shrug. "You?"

He shrugs as well. "I had to study him in school. Wordy, morose fucker."

"That just proves he's Irish."

His laughter is like a song. I want to keep him talking, so I ask, "You went to school? I thought all you London Beggars lived in an underground station."

"We do. I…" Now he hesitates, taking a sip of stout before answering, "I tested as gifted when I was young, so they sent me to a mundane school."

My heart falls, just a little. I knew he was too posh for me, even if he turns out to be gay, which he isn't. I can't let myself dream that big. All I want is to enjoy his company for a short while. It's not too much to ask, is it?

"You still in school?" I ask.

"I'm at uni."

University. I don't even want to know which one. Figures I'd set my eyes way too high. Time to change the subject before my heart breaks even more. "So, Abram, yeah? Aren't all the English Beggars named Abram?"

"We are. Just like Strowlers have bird names. Speaking of which, are you staying at the local Nest?"

I scoff. I should be more cautious, but I've downed half a pint to settle my nerves. "Yeah, but I want to move. The Upright Man was a friend of my father, and I know he's spying on me, telling my family what I'm up to."

"What are you up to that's so bad?"

"Nothing much. I'm not your typical Strowler, that's all." I take another sip. "I don't want to do physical labor or get into fist fights for prize money, or any of that macho shite. If I hadn't been hustling, I'd have been busking when you walked past today." With my wife, whose soulful fiddle, beautiful voice, and swollen belly had been earning us good gelt. "I also refurbish old scooters. I have a knack for it, going to the junkyard, finding a rusty heap and turning it into a vintage beauty. Been doing it since I was a kid."

"You're not still a kid?"

"What? No. I'm seventeen. A male Strowler becomes a man when he turns sixteen."

"What about the girls? When are they considered women?"

"The same." I can tell by his squint that this troubles him. He's probably heard the rumor that most Strowler girls are married at sixteen, like Bridie. I quickly ask, "When are Beggars considered adults?"

"When we're eighteen, both men and women."

That's the Crossroads standard. Anyone under the age of eighteen can't accept a challenge to fight or be held accountable for the actions of their family or clan, though each clan has its own laws within its ranks.

"I heard tell the Two Dragon Clan considers lads to be men when they turn fifteen."

Gareth sneers and mutters, "The Two Dragon Clan."

We clink glasses and drink. Every clan knows to be leery of them and their magic. "You ever meet any of them?"

"Not that I know of."

"Me, neither. Their powers sound amazing."

"They claim they got those powers from a dragon."

I lean forward. "Really? How? You mean, from a talking dragon?"

"Hell if I know. You don't believe that crap, do you?"

I shrug and smile, feeling bolder now that I've finished my pint. "What if I do?"

"I'd want to know more about you." His answering smile stabs my heart with the sweetest pain. "Another pint? My round."

"Ta." While he goes to the bar, I go to the loo to take a piss and splash cold water on my face. I need to slow down. Back off. With any luck, Shane will tell Gareth about Bridie while he's pulling our pints, and my game will be stashed.

When I get back to the table, those blue eyes are still gazing on me with the interest and attention I crave. My agony continues, and I'm determined to enjoy every minute.

So, I tell him the story of Master Stoorworm and Leannán Sidhe. He tells me why Beggars take the surname Abram. Back in the day, Beggars posed as former inmates of the Abraham ward of Bedlam Hospital. They'd sham lunacy to earn gelt and cover their true intentions, which usually involved spying.

"I know some songs about Tom of Bedlam and his wife, Mad Maud," I say.

"I'd like to hear you sing them."

There's nothing I'd like more than to sing for him. Well, maybe a few things. A blush creeps across my face. I wave a casual hand. "Ah, you'll be too busy. What are you doing here anyway, in the middle of the day? Shouldn't you be out begging?"

"I'm not your typical Beggar."

"That's right. You're at uni." I take a final swig from my glass, downing the contents, feeling the burn.

"And I'm gay."

I swallow hard, patting my chest to keep from choking. After I finish sputtering, I look at him with watering eyes. He knows. I just have to say it. I take courage from the alcohol singing in my blood.

"I'm gay, too."

And it's said. The words hang in the air, spoken. Can't be unsaid. Can't be undone. I can't be ungay. Nausea clenches my throat. I'm gay. Undeniably so. Every pretense I built came crashing down after a couple of pints with a bonny lad.

"Thought so." He finishes his pint and sets down his glass. "Another round?"

I shake my head slowly. I'm having a hard time keeping the contents of my stomach down. My eyes water and I take deep breaths.

"You all right, mate?"

I lick my dry lips so I can speak. "Yeah. It's just… I've told no one. Never said the words out loud."

Footsteps sound behind me. I spin around, expecting to see Oren holding a gun, ready as he has been all my life to end my life. Instead, it's just a couple of middle-aged women, carrying their glasses of wine to a nearby table. I take another deep breath, pressing my hand to my pounding heart.

Gareth lays his hand on my shoulder and squeezes. "Thank you for telling me."

I give a slight nod. I don't move, not wanting him to remove his hand and that sweet pressure on my shoulder which calms me.

"Is it bad among Strowlers?"

"Yeah," I say as a half-laugh, half-sob. "For me, it's a death sentence. My brother suspects and told me he'd kill me if I come out. Otherwise, it's shunning at the very least. I'd never find work or help among other Strowlers. At least, not those on the Glory Road. How is it among Beggars?"

"Well, I'm out, but we're in London. I might not be as free in another city."

"That's why I brought us here, so we could be more free."

"We?" Even as he says the word, my phone rings. I know who it is because she's bloody psychic. Gareth's smooth white brow crinkles and he smiles. "Is that your wife?"

My throat goes dry. I don't look away, but he can see it in my eyes. His hand slips from my shoulder. Then he sits back, arms folded, and gives a soft whistle. "Bloody hell. Does she know?"

I shake my miserable head.

"Can you tell her? I mean, will your life be in danger if you do?"

"Dunno."

"Do you care about her?"

"I love her. We're having a child."

He cocks his head. "Sure you're not bi?"

"I wish. No. I'm not attracted to her at all. It's not what she deserves."

"It's not what either of you deserve."

My brow crinkles. I thought what I deserved was a bullet in the head, but maybe not? "You don't think I'm trash?"

"No, of course not, but we're still on the Crossroads. Honor is everything. You can't cheat on her."

"I know. I wasn't going to. It's just… I wanted to talk to you. Maybe pretend there was a possibility, even though I knew there wasn't."

"You shouldn't lead other people on. There's no honor in that, either."

My ears burn. I duck my head as if that could hide my shame.

He nudges my arm. "It's all right. No hard feelings."

I look up into those blue eyes warmed with compassion and I know I can't lose him, even if I can't have him. "You fancy being mates?"

"What?"

"I don't know any other gay people."

His eyes narrow. Then he shrugs. "Sure. Yeah. We can be mates."

"Bridie, that's my wife, she and I are playing here on Friday night. You should come."

"Playing? You mean music, not a shell game?"

"Yeah, music. Come see us, yeah? She's got a beautiful voice."

He hesitates, as if considering whether he really wants to be mates with me. I could Charm him if I wanted, but I don't. If he doesn't want to be friends, that would only make it worse and me an even more miserable bastard.

"Sure. I'll bring Helena."

"You have a wife?"

"No, she's my older sister. She's on leave right now."

"That's right. You Beggars do military service."

"Can't be a Beggar unless you've been a soldier, except for rare exceptions."

"Are you one of those exceptions?"

He shakes his head. "The military is paying for me to go to uni to become a doctor. Once I graduate, I'm theirs."

A doctor. He really is too posh for me. I'm glad Bridie called. Everything's out in the open and maybe, just maybe, I really have an actual friend.

Dream

GERRY

When I get home, I tell Bridie the truth, that a Beggar lad came to my aid during a shell game gone wrong, and I took him out for a couple of pints.

She's eager to meet Gareth and his sister, and doesn't say why, though I know. She's lonely. Too different to make friends with the women at this Nest, just as I can't connect with the men. We should've left months ago, but no flock invited us to join their Flight.

Before bed that night, I give her a massage, easing the strain in her muscles from late pregnancy. Her skin is smooth and lovely, and touching her fills me with tenderness and love, and that's it. Why isn't that enough? We go to bed and she nestles against me. I curl my arm around her, close my eyes, and think about what Gareth smelled like. Leather with a hint of sharpness, like whisky…

Our child stirs beneath my hand. Oren is right. I am a piece of shit, thinking of someone else while holding my pregnant wife. I close my eyes, banishing thoughts of him, and his touch, and what could have been. Tears fill my eyes. Somehow, I manage not to sob.

I drift from our caravan in London, gliding through the night sky, above the land, across the sea, to a cove on the Isle of Wight, where Master Stoorworm lays coiled around the boulders at his leisure.

"Look, you, what'd you want from me?" I ask.

"What I want is almost accomplished."

Accomplished? "What the feck is that supposed to mean?" I think for a moment. "You mean Bridie's pregnancy? Are you talking about our child? You want our child?"

The scales open and close over his glowing red eyes in a lazy wink. "What would I want with a human child?"

"I don't know. You tell me."

He doesn't, of course.

"Look, you can't have my kid, yeah? Over my dead body."

"Your body, dead or alive, cannot stop me from gaining what I will."

"Stay away from my family."

"Your family has nothing to fear from me."

If only I could believe that.

PENNY

Helena coaxes Bridie into the kitchen and Kai and I convince a couple of bites of toast and some black coffee down her throat. When a spark of life returns to her dull eyes, Helena tells her about the phone number.

Bridie shakes her head, winces, and presses her fingers into her forehead. "She won't talk to me. None of them will. His family hates me."

"I can call." Helena offers.

"No. They can't suspect any relationship between Gerry and Gareth. It could be the death of him." She nods at Gareth, who's leaning against the kitchen counter.

"What if they do?" he asks. "Gerry and I were about to come out, anyway."

"And now he's gone." Bridie grabs hold of Helena's forearm. "I told my brother we're taking refuge here because you and I are friends. No one can know it's for any other reason. Not if you don't want your brother to die."

"I'm Mad Maud," she replies calmly. "No one dares harm him. But I understand your fear."

I hold back an impatient huff. We can't let our only lead fizzle. "I'll call her."

The adults exchange uneasy glances before giving reluctant nods.

I suck in air between my gritted teeth as I tap the number onto my screen. Then I set the phone on the table, speaker on, and we listen to the rings.

"Yeah?" It's a woman's voice, rough with age and grief.

My stomach roils. I clear my throat and say, "Hi. This is Penny. Gerry's daughter. Can we talk? I…"

The line goes dead.

Fine. I didn't want to talk to her, anyway. Some grandmother she turned out to be. I don't know her, I've never met her, but right now I absolutely hate her.

Bridie throws her hands in the air. "See, they won't talk to us. Not even her, and she's innocent."

"Mum, none of you were guilty."

She scoffs. "Tell them that."

The phone rings. The screen shows the same number I just dialed. We all freeze, all but Kai, who reaches across the table and taps the screen.

I want to tell her to sod off. Instead, I say a cautious, "Hello?"

"This Penny?" It's a man's voice, harsh and bullying even with those two words. I recognize it immediately even though I haven't seen him in three years.

Bridie does, too, and covers her mouth to stifle her gasp.

I breathe through my pounding heart and say, "Yes."

"This is Oren Kestrel. Don't call me uncle. You're no blood of mine. Everyone knows your mother's a whore, though I can scarce blame her, seeing how her family married her off to a Sodomite."

A red haze covers my eyes and I bite my lip bloody to keep from calling him an evil motherfucker. I sit on my hands to keep from hanging up.

"Gerry's missing. Do you know what happened to him?"

"Of course, I know. He's dead."

Those two words. My greatest fear. Through the buzzing in my ears, I hear my mother's muffled shriek and my brother's audible cry.

No. Don't believe it. Challenge him.

"How did he die?"

"Dunno. His body was dumped in front of the London Nest. They didn't leave a calling card. Eddie Lark, the Upright Man, called and told me what happened, so I came and collected the body."

That sounds too right. Too verifiable. Can it be true? Can Gerry really be dead? No, no, he's lying. He must be. I'm trembling, so I take a deep breath to steady my voice.

"Why didn't you tell us?"

"Why should I? Your mother's dallying with a Two Dragon Clan gull, and you're not our kin. What business is it of yours?"

How dare he talk to me like that?

"What business? I'm his daughter. I demand to see his body."

He scoffs. "The only reason I'm calling is because Mammy told me you're innocent in all this and deserve to know. So, here it is. I collected his body, took him to the morgue, had him cremated, and spread his ashes on the crossroads. That's it. Done. Out of our lives and yours as well. You should thank me. He did you no service, claiming to be your father. If you want no further grief from us, tell your mother to be decent for once in her life and return to the Sparrow Nest. Now, it's your turn. Tell me who he was committing sodomy with. I want the names of the man or men, more like, so I can put things to right."

I slam my hand on the screen to stop his evil screed. Then I snatch up the phone and block the number so neither Oren Kestrel nor his weak excuse for a mother can call me back.

I look up to see Bridie and Kai holding each other tight, tears flowing as wails erupt from their throats.

Auntie Helena is holding her brother, but he's stiff and still as a statue. Then he blinks and says in a harsh tone, "I don't believe it. Oren's always had it out for Gerry. He'd happily lie about his death if it meant hurting anyone he loves. I'm going to find him and beat the fucking truth out of him."

"No, you're not and that's an order," she replies firmly. "The Beggars and Strowlers in Ulster are close allies, and Oren Kestrel is the Upright Man of his Nest. You can't cause hostility between our clans." She takes a breath. "Now, what I can do is call in a favor with Eddie Lark."

"You already called him," snaps Gareth. "And he lied to you."

"Yeah, but since we've heard from Oren Kestrel, he might be more open to talk. I'll also check the CCTV in the area around the Nest…"

Bridie shakes her head vehemently. "Why? What's the point? He's gone. Gone. Both my lovely lads, gone." With a keening wail, she collapses onto the table.

Kai curls into a tight ball, pressing his forehead to his knees. Helena sits beside him, wrapping her arms around him.

Gareth and I reach for each other's hand and squeeze hard. Gerry can't be dead. I still feel him.

Unless he only lives in my dreams.

Dream

PENNY

We Strowlers have a belief about burials. We consider death to be our journey's end and have cemeteries where our people are laid to rest. If someone among us has been guilty of the worst crimes, we spread their ashes at the crossroads, dooming them to endless wandering without rest.

That's what Oren did to Gerry.

Now I can't rest. I wander the Abode, moving without stopping, close to the walls, staring straight ahead, trying to be invisible. Ghost-like. Maybe if I can be emotionless, weightless, and spare, I'll encounter Gerry's spirit. He must be here. Where else would he be?

I save the atrium for last because it's the most obvious place and if he's not there, he's nowhere.

Back in the day, Gray Cloak Station had two entrances, including one with a glass ceiling. The Beggars turned it into a secret garden with trees, grass, flowering plants, and even a waterfall fountain that feeds into a stream. I'd come here with

Gerry and Gareth, just the three of us, and we'd have picnics, and I'd feel special.

My feet crunch on the gravel path as I make my way to one of the long marble benches in front of the fountain. Weary grief weighs me down so that I can't sit. Instead, I lay on my side, resting my head on my forearm. A watery mist envelopes me. I close my eyes.

Da, are you here? Please, please talk to me.

Nothing.

I should get up and go back to the train, but I don't want to move. The sound of the fountain soothes me. I concentrate on the steady flow of falling water and let go.

The bench sways beneath me in a rolling motion. I'm on a boat. I open my eyes and lift my head. It's the ferry from Dover to Dunkirk. We're heading for Amsterdam to play in the pubs there. We parked our caravan in the hold and we're on the upper deck, breathing in the fresh air and looking at the stars, even though it's cold.

Gerry and Matthew sit shoulder to shoulder. Matthew has his arm around Bridie and she's cuddling Kai. I'm snuggled against Gerry, warm and content, my head on his shoulder.

"Where are you, Da?" I ask.

He gives me his sideways grin, a twinkle in those blue eyes. "Where I always am, darling. Snatching defeat from the jaws of victory."

"What does that mean?"

"Nothing. Don't pay me any mind. You're my lucky Penny. Always have been since the day you were born."

"But…"

"Shh." He presses a kiss to my forehead and holds me closer. Then he sings in a soft voice that has an odd, bubbly tone, almost as if he was underwater.

> "Sleep on, sleep on my green-eyed treasure,
> Oh, my wandering days will soon be done.
> See how those London Lights are shining
> Through the frost and falling snow.
> Sleep on, sleep on my green-eyed treasure,
> Oh, your father's got nowhere to go."

Past

GERRY

"It's a girl."

Three words that change my world.

I'm terrified, of course, but also relieved. I don't want a son, partly for fear that Oren will get hold of him and turn him against me. Mainly, because the worst part of my life was being a son and a brother. I want to spare my child my fate, and that's easier with a lass than a lad.

I hold the babe while the nurses tend to Bridie, my hand still aching from the grip of her labor. I tried to be the best husband possible, rubbing her back, stroking her hair, wiping her brow, murmuring encouraging words and shutting up when she told me to sod off.

Now this little wain is ours. So fragile. I'm afraid of dropping her or doing anything that will damage her. Can I keep her safe for the rest of her life? Is that even possible? No. I'll do everything in my power to make her strong and independent.

A mighty girl. But how do I do that when I'm a weak man living a lie?

By being honest with her and her mother.

The babe's eyelids flutter open, and I gasp.

"What is it?" asks Bridie, pushing away a nurse.

"She has blue eyes."

My wife huffs as she lays back on the pillows. "You gave me a start."

The nurse chuckles. "All babies are born with either blue or brown eyes. They could turn green, but it'll be a few months."

"I hope they turn green. Just like her mother's." I stroke the soft, dark, downy strands atop the baby's head before carefully handing her back to Bridie. Tears fill her eyes as she cuddles our child, kisses her cheeks, and strokes her soft skin. Then she looks up, her emerald eyes sparkling with joy and love as she beams on me.

I am the worst man in the world.

A nurse brandishes a Polaroid camera and chirps, "Family photo."

I settle on the bed beside my wife, curling my arm around her. She cuddles against me, proudly cradling our daughter at the best angle for the camera. I smile and hope the panic doesn't show in my eyes. While the nurse waves the photo around to air dry it, Bridie settles against me, sighing contently.

"I love you," she whispers.

"I love you, too," I whisper back, meaning every word. That's the worst part. I love her. I'm tied to her, I want to be shut of her, but I also want to spend my life with her and raise our child together.

What the hell am I going to do?

Bridie nudges me. "Where are you?"

I give my head a little shake and add an apologetic smile. "Just thinking about everything."

She gets that hurt look in her eyes, because I'm always distant and she doesn't understand why. "I said you need to call our families."

"Yeah, yeah." I kiss her cheek, pat the babe's head, and slide off the bed and out the door. Once I'm in the corridor, I realize I didn't stop and gaze back at her lovingly. I'm a shite husband, no doubt. She deserves far better.

I go outside to clear my head and have a smoke. It takes only one cigarette before I'm ready to call Bridie's family. As expected, they offer hearty congratulations and express their eagerness to see the new Sparrow.

It takes two more cigarettes before I work up the nerve to call my mother.

"Yeah," she answers in a voice that speaks of being ground down to nothing but a wary shadow.

"Hi, Mammy. It's me. Gerry."

"So it is. What'd you want?"

"Just wanted to let you know the babe's been born. It's a girl. We named her Penny."

"Ah. Well. Good for you, then."

"Would you like to see her?"

"I suppose I would, but I can't. Oren's been telling everyone your wife whored herself, at your urging, so's to give birth to a bastard you can claim as your own."

It's as though she poured hot coals on my head. Rage sears my flesh. I yell as though on fire, "That's a fucking lie!"

"Don't matter. Oren don't want you here, don't want to see your wife or child. He says you're a molly, and no child will make that any different."

I hang up to keep from yelling she's a spineless mort who never lifted a finger to defend me against my brothers. I lean against the brick wall and heave a long sigh. My only memories of my father are of him beating her. Maybe that's when she defended me until he broke her.

The worst thing is Oren's right. I am a molly and having a child can't change that.

I go to Mumpers Hall that night because it's what's expected of me. A group of Strowlers from the Nest are there to pound my back, offer me cigars, and ply me with whiskey. The hall is crowded, the music loud, and I'm content to lean against the bar and disappear in other people's joy. Then a familiar presence glides up beside me. I don't have to see him to know who it is. I could happily drown in the musky scent of him.

"All right." Gareth nods at me before nodding at the barmaid and holding up one finger.

"All right, mate," I reply. "Not buying one for the new father?"

"Looks like you've had enough."

"Yes, Da." When the barmaid sets down his pint, I motion for her to pour me the same.

"On me," Gareth tells her. "How's your wife and child?"

"Ah, grand. Bridie's strong. She dropped the babe in record time, according to the midwife. It's a girl. We named her Penny."

"Congratulations." We clink glasses. He takes a sip. "Why Penny?"

"Bridie loves the Beatles, and I'm keen on them as well. We decided if it was a girl, we'd name her Penny Lane."

"What if it was a boy?"

"Ringo Starr." I look at his incredulous face and laugh. "I'm glad I'm married to her and not you. You're no bloody fun."

"Not so loud," he whispers.

"Maybe that's the problem," I say, though I lower my voice. "I'm not loud enough. I let everyone walk all over me and now here I am. A father. I decided, though. I'm going to tell her."

"Tell Bridie that you're…"

"Yeah."

"When?"

"Not this very moment. I'm not that much of a prat. I'll wait until she's recovered. When are you off to uni?"

"September 10."

I give a resolute nod. "That's my deadline. I'll do it before then because I want you here. I need you here."

"I'll be here. It's just… are you sure?"

"More than sure. I can lie to myself, but I can't lie to my child, and I'm done lying to Bridie. Whatever happens afterward, I'll take it on the chin and carry on. But I'll need you here. Really."

"And I'll be here for you, really. But it has to be before the tenth."

"It will. On my honor."

Gareth whistles softly. Honor is everything on the Crossroads. By saying such, it means I can't take it back. I set my course. All I have to do now is find the right time.

So, it turns out there's no right time when you have a newborn. Days fold into each other as I help my exhausted wife with our child. Bridie's breastfeeding and Penny's a greedy little wain, waking us up in the wee hours to be fed. I don't work my shell game or any other dodgy shams. Instead, I stay in the Nest and refurbish the junked scooters I've been collecting. It's an honest, if not lucrative living, and I'm making enough reselling for us to get by.

When I'm done for the day, I go back into the caravan and take the baby while Bridie takes a shower and gets some sleep. I cradle my daughter while eating dinner, and in between bites tell her tales of how she's my princess and I'll always protect her from the dragon.

Who am I kidding? I can protect her all I want from my dream dragon, but how do I keep her safe from the monster of my nightmares, Oren? Will the truth protect her or make her more of a target?

Neither. Oren's made up his mind about me, and it doesn't matter how many wains I make with Bridie.

September 8 arrives like an unwelcome in-law. I can't put it off anymore. Gareth will go to Oxford if I don't do it now. I need him here, with me, to fall in love proper-like, and help me learn how to be gay on the Crossroads. After breakfast, I do the dishes while Bridie nurses Penny. When she's done, I take Penny from her arms and settle beside her. Bridie rests her head on my shoulder with a long, content sigh.

"I'm the luckiest lass as ever was. There's nary a Strowler man that helps his wife with the children. Why are you so wonderful?"

"I'm not really." As I say those words, I hold my daughter tighter. What if I'm never allowed to see her again? If I hadn't given Gareth my word of honor, my nerve would fail me, and I'm really wishing I hadn't right now.

"Don't be daft," says she, snuggling a little closer.

"Bridie, there's something I need to tell you."

She stiffens. Looks up. A tentative smile forms on her lips, wanting it to be a joke. Then our eyes meet. Her smile fades. She sucks in her breath and leaves the shelter of my embrace.

"What?" she whispers.

I swallow once. Twice. Breathe. How do I say it? By just saying it. "I'm gay."

We stare at each other, her green eyes fathomless. It's shock.

Once that's worn off, she'll give me what for. Then she leans back, pressing her hand to her chest.

"Oisin told me you're a molly, and not to marry you. I told him I didn't care. That living in our Nest was killing me and I needed to get out. After we… after the beach, I wanted to believe that you weren't really gay, or you were bi and loved me enough that you chose me. But you didn't, did you? You married me because you had to, to hide what you are."

"I love you. I thought it would be enough to change me. It's not. I'm gay and I can't not be, and I don't want to keep lying to you."

Fear fills her eyes. "Are you going to leave me?"

"No. I want to raise our child with you. I don't know how that will work. If it can work, but I do love you, Bridie. And I love our child more than the world. I'll do anything to make it up to you."

"Except be my husband," she whispers, realization dawning on her face. "That's why you avoided sex so much. I thought it was because my pregnancy repulsed you. But it was me. I repulsed you."

"It's not that." How do I explain? Just by saying it. "I can't make myself feel desire for a woman, any woman. I thought I could be with you because of how I feel about you, but it doesn't work like that."

She shakes her head. "You're a fecking eejit. And so am I."

"I'm sorry. So, so sorry. I never should've touched you. This is all my fault."

Bridie tugs Penny out of my arms. "I need to think. Can you go away for a while? Come back… I don't know. Tomorrow."

I nod numbly. "Do you need anything?"

"I need you to leave." Her voice breaks. She bows her head over the baby and her shoulders shake. Between sobs, she gasps out, "Now."

I grab my jacket and helmet and leave, closing the front door behind me with a soft click. Then I stand there, staring into space like a simpleton. My life exploded and the pieces are everywhere, and I don't have a clue how to put things back together.

Gareth meets me at the Plough and Stars, where I'm sitting at our table, working on my third pint of bitters.

"All right," he says.

I don't reply. He puts his arm across my shoulders, and I lean into his lean, muscular strength. I long to rest my head on his chest, but I can't. Not only because I don't want to be seen. I can't do that to Bridie. Cheat on her right after telling her.

"You don't understand. Bridie was the best thing that ever happened to me. Before her, I was my family's punching bag. She's my first real friend, and I lied to her the whole time. The worst part is I love her and our child. I don't want to lose them."

"You don't have to lose them. Bridie's special. She didn't care I was gay when she met me."

"You're not married to her."

"Fair enough. But she's not hateful, and she needs you."

"That's what else I've done to her. If she goes back to her family with a child in tow, she'll be considered a burden and married off to the next man who wants her."

"Does she know that?"

"Yeah."

"Then let her decide what she wants to do. I don't think you give her enough credit."

"Maybe not," I whisper. "And then there's me. I don't know how to be gay. Especially not on the Crossroads."

He squeezes my shoulder. "I'll help you when I'm here."

I pull away. "What do you mean when you're here?"

"I'm going to Oxford in two days, you know that."

"I thought... I thought if I came out to Bridie, you'd stay."

He sighs and shakes his head. "Ah, Gerry. No, I can't. I'm in the Beggar Clan, on the Glory Road, and given my orders. I go to university, become a doctor, and do my military service. It'll be at least ten years before I return to the Abode full time."

Ten. Years. It takes all my strength not to bury my head in my arms and weep. I blew up my life for a man who can't be with me. Thing is, I knew it. Deep down. I'm not that thick. I just didn't want to believe it.

"How can I do this without you?"

"I'll come on the weekends when I can. Look, I know I talked you into this. I won't abandon you. On my honor."

Those three words lift my soul. He's pledged himself to me, at least to help me. I'm not losing him. I'm not alone.

"Bridie kicked me out until tomorrow. I don't know where to go."

"You can stay in the Abode tonight."

"I can? How?"

"Strowlers and Beggars are allies. It should be all right. I'll text Helena."

"And I'll get another drink."

It's two more drinks before I stagger out the door of the pub. The fresh air hits my face and for a moment, I feel better. Then my eyes water as my gut churns and I lurch into the alley. I brace myself against the wall as vomit pours out of me like hot lava. My legs feel like jelly, but I stay upright. When I'm finally done, my stomach feels better, but my head is worse. I wipe away the vomit, snot, and tears on my sleeve.

Despite that, Gareth puts my arm across his shoulders, wraps his arm around my waist, and leads me through the alley.

Ah, now this is grand. Why hadn't I thought of this before? Falling down drunk is the perfect excuse to be close to him and feel the friction of his body against mine.

"Are you going to have your way with me?" I mumble.

"Not tonight."

"I don't blame you. I'm a hot mess."

"That you are."

No one pays us any mind as we weave through the streets. London is full of drunks on a Friday night. Everything becomes fuzzy and blurry. I close my eyes but still move my feet, allowing him to steer me wherever he will. I don't care, so long as I'm with him.

We stop in front of the entrance to an abandoned underground station. I close my eyes again as Gareth talks to someone who doesn't sound as though he's going to let me in. I swallow to moisten my mouth so I can tell Gareth it's all right. He can dump me off on a park bench. I've slept on plenty, so I wouldn't have to sleep in the same caravan as Oren.

Oren, who would come to my bed when everyone was asleep and touch me.

No.

No. I don't think about that. Never.

I focus on another voice. A female one. Helena. She tells the guard who stopped us to allow me in, and that's that.

God, I love a strong woman. A strong man, too. I know I'll love Gareth until the day I die.

We move again, but all I can concentrate on is his arm around my waist and how secure it makes me feel. I never want him to let me go, except he does, to lower me onto a bench.

My eyes blink open. We're in a park, after all. Disappointment tightens my chest, even though I don't blame him. Why would the Beggars allow a drunken sod like me into their forbidden Abode?

I look up, squinting at the glass ceiling. "Where are we?"

"The atrium," says Gareth, his hand on my shoulder to keep me upright. "An indoor garden. It's part of the Abode."

"The fuck?" I glance around at the fountain burbling behind us and the foliage creeping up the walls. I close my eyes and breathe in the earthy scent, clearing some of the muck from my head.

"Gerry."

I blink to clear my vision.

Helena stands before me, hands on her hips, and a frown on her lips. "I talked to Bridie. She told me everything."

"She aright?" I slur out. "She and the baby. My baby… I'm a piece of shite. She tell you?"

"She's very upset. I'm going to see her. You need to get your "shite" together and be the man she needs you to be right now."

"I'm gay. I can't stop that."

"No, you can't, but she still needs you." She turns to her brother. "He has to stay in here until morning and you have to stay with him." She nods toward a bench that has pillows and blankets.

"There a loo?" I ask.

"Behind the fountain to the left."

I stand and stay steady enough on my feet to wobble my way to the men's room. I take a long piss and then a long drink from the faucet before scrubbing my face. My reflection in the mirror winces back at me. Hot mess is too kind a phrase to describe me.

Back in the atrium, Helena's gone. Gareth's already stretched out on one bench. I lay down on the other one so that we're head-to-head. The pillow and blanket feel like luxuries. I glance around and see glowing red dots at random locations on the walls.

"Are we being watched?" I whisper.

"Yes," he whispers back.

"Can they hear us?"

"They're not supposed to."

I stare at the night sky through the glass ceiling. A handful of stars wink their way through the haze of the city's lights. "I wish I was a Beggar."

"Do you?"

I think for a moment. "Nah. I don't fancy myself a soldier."

"The Irish Beggars don't join the military."

The Irish Beggars don't have you. I don't say that aloud. I might as well wish myself into university since it's just as likely to happen. "Nah. I'm Strowler for better or worse. I can't imagine myself not traveling."

I'm hoping he's going to say more. I want to stay up all night and talk, but I'm so weary and dizzy, and sad, but also happy. How can I sleep?

But I do.

The dragon weaves his way through my dreams, soaring across the land before diving into the sea. Another dragon joins him, this one smaller, wingless, with blue scales and an opalescent glow on his chest. They circle each other, bubbles pouring from their snouts. Then they see me and stop, their long serpentine bodies bobbing with the tide, as they stare at me, expecting something. What? I don't know. Only that they're not done with me yet.

I wake up with an aching head and the morning sun in my eyes. Birds twitter away on the tree branches. Real birds. Is it cruel of the Beggars to keep them inside? Or are they free to come and go, and choose to stay? I wish I had that choice.

Gareth is gone, though his bedding remains. I know better than to look for him, so I head for the loo. Cold water is fucking awful first thing in the morning after a binge, but it wakes me up, and I splash around and towel off until I'm semi-presentable. Gareth is waiting on the bench, with a pot of coffee and a plate of scones.

"Cheers," I say, taking the mug he holds out. I sit and take a long, dark sip. Neither my stomach nor heart are in the mood for cream and sugar. I skip the jam and butter, preferring my scone plain as my life is about to become.

"All right?" he asks, that smooth white brow wrinkling with concern.

I shake my head.

"What will you do if Bridie outs you?"

"Run for it. Change my name. Plant myself somewhere and not come back until… well… ever."

He runs a hand through that thick, gorgeous hair. "Jesus, Gerry, I… I'm sorry. I shouldn't have talked you into it."

"It's all right. It was killing me inside. I feel alive again. My only regret will be my daughter. I want to be there for her."

"I didn't realize it was that bad."

I shrug.

"All because you're gay." He shakes his head. "It's the twenty-first century…"

"Not on the Crossroads. You know that. You're just lucky you were born into a clan that doesn't care." My phone buzzes in my jacket pocket. I pull it out and see Bridie's name on the screen. My stomach clenches around the coffee and scone. It takes all my strength to tap the screen. "Hello?"

"Helena told me where you spent the night." She sounds tired, spiritless. "I'm glad you're somewhere safe. I'm sorry I kicked you out. I… I… needed to think."

"It's all right, love," I whisper.

"Love," she whispers back. "I loved you." Her voice cracks. "I still do."

"I love you, too." Tears fill my eyes. "I want to see you and Penny."

"Then come home."

"I will. I'll be right there." I hang up and exhale. "She wants me to come back."

"Good. Whatever happens, I'm here for you, yeah?" His thumb gently brushes away the tears that rolled down my cheeks.

I turn my face toward his and close my eyes, praying that I haven't misread him, that I don't have to beg. His lips touch mine gently. His unshaven chin scrapes my skin in the most tantalizing way. I open my mouth like a baby bird, wanting so much more. His tongue winds with mine. My blood sings and my heart soars. I never want this to end. The smell of him, his hands gripping my arms, his chest pressing against mine.

Someone clears their throat.

We break apart.

Helena stands before us, hands on her hips. She's dressed as a Beggar rather than a soldier, wearing a ragged plaid shirt tied at her waist and a voluminous patched skirt over battered combat boots. She's shorter than her brother and has the same blue eyes, though with a steely glint that won't be messed with.

"I spent the night with your wife and child," she announces.

My face burns, but not from shame or regret. I'd kiss Gareth a hundred… a thousand… a million more times and take whatever happens. "Thanks," I mumble.

"You can thank me by going home."

"I will. I'm on my way."

"I'll walk him out," says Gareth.

"No." His sister pins him in place with her gaze. "I'll do it."

I glance over my shoulder as I follow her out of the Atrium, keeping my eyes on him as long as I can. I'll see him again, but at what cost? Why must I be so torn?

As I steer through the Nest on my scooter, a group of men look up from the truck engine they're bent over and side-eye me while chugging from their beer cans. Women peer out at me through the curtains of their caravans. God knows what they're cackling about us. I'm sure a Beggar woman spending the night with Bridie didn't help. To hell with them. Whatever happens, I'm done with this place.

Inside our caravan, I find Bridie in bed, breastfeeding Penny. She looks up as I enter the room and her gaze isn't angry or reproachful. It's sad and weary. I did this to her. I saddled her with a child to prove my manhood. Now Gareth's kiss fills me with shame. I shouldn't have come out. I should've steered clear of him, stayed with my wife and child, and been a proper Strowler, at least until they don't need me anymore. But when will that be? Don't they deserve the truth, sooner than later?

I don't know.

"You look the dog's dinner," says Bridie as she lifts Penny onto her shoulder and starts patting her back.

I reach out automatically because burping's my job. She hands me the baby without hesitation. I sit on the edge of the bed and breathe in my daughter's milky sweetness. Tears well up in my eyes. I don't want to lose her.

"Helena came over last night. She brought a bottle of wine and a pizza. We talked for hours. It felt good, having a friend I can say anything to. I thought I had that with you."

"You do. You can tell me anything, Bridie."

"Then why didn't you tell me before we got... involved?"

I take a breath because I need to think for a moment. It was fear, of course, but it was more than that. "Because you were the first girl I had feelings for. Really, you're the first friend I've ever had. I thought... hoped I could be straight for you so we could be together. I wanted to be with you. I still do."

"But not in bed?"

I shake my head. "I can't feel what you need me to feel to be together in that way. It's not you. It's any woman. I'm not… I can't…" I give a frustrated half shrug with my free shoulder. "I'm gay."

"Do you feel that way about Gareth?"

I'm done lying, so I nod yes.

She sucks in a breath. "Last night, did you and he… do it?"

I shake my head. "I haven't had sex with anyone but you."

"And that's done. What do you want?"

"I don't want to lose you and the baby, but I don't want to live a lie. I don't know what that looks like. What do you want? Do you want to go home?"

"This is my home. I'm not going back to the Nest in disgrace. If I do that, what happens to you? It'd be like putting a target on your back. Plus, I'm done with all this," she waves her hands, "Glory Road shite. I'm tired of those cows tutting at me and saying it's time to settle down and be a proper wife. The only way this is going to work is if we walk the Wayward Way."

My heart lifts at those words. "You mean it?"

"I wouldn't say it if I didn't. I want out of here. Now. Right now. I don't care where we go. Liverpool, maybe. Stay in the Wayward Way Nest to establish ourselves. And we'll figure out how this works between us."

My mouth dries. I don't want to leave right now, not without seeing Gareth one more time, but I have no excuse. I sold my last scooter yesterday, which she well knows. How can I deny her this after she's saved my life? The baby senses my emotion and starts fussing against my shoulder. Bridie reaches out and I hand Penny to her.

"I need to take a nap before the drive."

She bites her lip before speaking, her voice becoming small. "Not in here."

"No. I'll move into the cab-over."

I collect the pillow on my side of the bed, gathering it against the pain stabbing my chest. Bridie ducks her head, her shoulders shaking as she cradles Penny. I want to comfort her, but what can I say that will make it any better? Not a damn thing.

I leave what was our room and climb into the cab-over. It's one big mattress, bedding already in place because Strowlers believe in being hospitable at a moment's notice. I close the curtains, lay in the dark, and tap out my tale to Gareth on my phone. Then I close my eyes and feel the buzz of his response against my chest. I don't want to look. Not yet. All I want to do right now is cry, and mourn, and hope.

Dream

GERRY

I'm a contrary bastard. You tell me to do something, I'll do the opposite. I can't help myself. I drink and smoke more than I should, but I could give up both if needed. Being perverse, though, that's my drug. My veins crave it. I need it in my blood and my soul. Maybe it's from all those years being bottled up by my family, suppressing everything that's truly me. After the top came off, I boiled over. I didn't care what anyone thought, until I had no choice.

Everyone knows it. At least, everyone I love and hate. Then there's this dragon. I don't know if I love or hate him. Maybe both. He wants to keep me with him in his jeweled cavern under the sea. I want to be with my family and the man I love. The more I fight, the more he closes me in, overpowering me, forcing me into a shell of his making.

He's a lot like Oren in that way.

Does he also want me dead?

All I can do is fight against them to stay alive.

Unless it's too late.

Past

PENNY

I met Oren Kestrel once, when I was 12 years old. I have no other memory of Gerry's family. Our parents only spoke of them in whispers.

Bridie's family, while not best pleased with her, adores me and my brother, and we're always made to feel welcome. Strowlers are matrilineal, so Kai and I are Sparrows, not Kestrels, and considered part of our nan's Nest outside Dublin. She's a Mother Bird, a Strowler woman who ceases her travels to keep a Nest that offers safe haven. This might sound feminist, but believe me, it's not. Strowler women hold the Nest's honor and must keep themselves pure and above reproach. The Mother Bird's husband, the Upright Man, rules the roost. How upright he is depends on the man.

Which brings me to Oren Kestrel.

The whispers always involved him and, from what I could overhear, he was the reason I'd never met Gerry's family. And why we'd never traveled to Ulster.

One day, Gerry announced Wild Sky had been invited to perform at the Lisnaskea Music Festival, replacing another band who'd had to cancel. I'd clapped my hands with joy because music festivals were easy gigs that pay well. Bridie and Matthew greeted the news with tight lips and side eyes. I opened the map app on my phone and saw that Lisnaskea was located across the border in Northern Ireland.

That night, I laid awake in my bunk, straining to overhear the whispers that started as soon as they thought Kai and I were asleep.

Matthew: What are you thinking? You know we can't go to Ulster.

Gerry: Who says we can't? What's the point of being on the Wayward Way if you don't go where you please?

Matthew: Don't be thick.

Bridie: He thinks he's being clever.

Gerry: I am. Oren doesn't own Ulster.

Bridie: You tell him that.

Gerry: He can fuck right off. Look, this isn't the kind of gig we can turn down. We're near skint. And Kelsey, Chelsea, whatever the fuck her name is, the producer, she can book us for future events. We need a connection like her.

Bridie: But if Oren finds out…

Gerry: He won't. How will he? Kelsey told me it's too late to add our name to the website. We'll be performing on the smallest stage. We'll be done and gone in a flash.

Matthew: How much are they paying again?

I chanced a peep through the curtain. Gerry was showing Matthew something on his phone screen.

Matthew softly whistled before turning to Bridie. "He's right. We can't turn that down."

Mum folded her arms and shook her head, but said no more.

Strowlers raise women to defer to men in all things monetary. Gerry and Matthew raised me differently, but that didn't keep them from using that to their advantage when it came to her.

The next day, we took the ferry from Liverpool to Dublin. Even I knew it would've been faster to cross to Belfast, but that wasn't an option. We spent the night at a Bleater caravan site to throw off the scent and left before dawn, driving for a few hours until we crossed the border into Ulster.

I had my nose pressed to the window, expecting it to be different from normal Ireland, but all I saw were the same rolling green hills dotted with sheep.

I wondered about Oren Kestrel. Why did he hate Gerry so much that none of us dare set foot in his precious Ulster? I couldn't imagine hating Kai like that, no matter what he'd done.

Despite these uneasy thoughts, I dozed off and didn't awaken until we pulled into the VIP parking lot of the Lisnaskea Festival. Fear of Oren Kestrel faded as my parents tuned their instruments and I put on my rig, a bedazzled, satin green dress, petticoats, lace shorts and lamb-legged socks, with hard tap shoes.

A knock on the door sounded like thunder throughout our caravan. Everyone froze, except Kai, who ran to the door and threw it open before anyone could stop him.

A young woman with pink hair and massive eyebrows poked her head in. "Hi, I'm Moira. Chelsea sent me. I'm to lead you to your set."

Sighs of relief gusted off the walls. Loud enough that Moira's brow pinched.

Gerry's easy smile appeared. "Stall the ball, love. We'll pack our kit and be right out."

Her eyebrows lifted away the pinch. "You from Ulster?"

He nods.

"You sound it."

"You, too." His smile faded as she closed the door behind her.

Why did he suddenly look sad? Strowlers aren't from anywhere really, though most had a home Nest, one they flocked to in the winter or time of need. Gerry's was a Kestrel Nest outside Belfast, just as Bridie's was a Sparrow Nest near Dublin. Walking the Wayward Way meant forsaking those Nests, which was why London was the closest thing we had to home.

Moira led us along the outer perimeter of the festival to our stage. I carried my penny whistles and Kai's bodhrán since the guitar case he hauled was almost as big as him. Our parents walked ahead of us, discussing last-minute adjustments to our set. Pride swelled my chest. They looked so flash with Gerry and Matthew in plaid shirts with ripped skinny jeans rolled above their Doc Marten boots, and Bridie wearing a fringed black bikini top, a denim miniskirt, and white trainers. Proper rock stars, they were. Then I noticed Moira's side eye, sizing up the parents and the children, and her lips twisting with that smirk of realization. I knew everyone thought Bridie shared her bed with both Gerry and

Matthew, and that they let everyone think that. Inside our caravan, it was clear Bridie and Matthew were married. The only person I'd seen Gerry kiss was Gareth, but that was a secret.

We were the first show of the day on that stage, replacing another family show. The kids in the audience eyed me and Kai with envy, and my chest swelled. We didn't have a house, or money, or even much schooling, but we had this, something they could only dream of. I wondered if Gerry noticed, too, since he did one last song change, and had Kai play the opening solo for Gypsy Rover. Matthew beamed at his son with pride before joining in.

Really, we were the best family. Anyone could see that if they'd stop judging.

Our set lasted half-an-hour, so I danced only twice. We left the stage to enthusiastic applause and quickly packed our instruments. The plan was to head back to the caravan and scarper, but Chelsea herself was waiting backstage, a middle-aged woman with bright red hair and lips, and enormous glasses. She peered at Gerry like he was a Cornetto she hoped to devour. She handed him vouchers for us to the VIP pavilion and told him to meet her there for a drink at two.

Regret filled his features. "Ah, that'd be grand, Chelsea, but we were planning to leave straight away."

"You can't leave. The VIP access road is closed until two a.m. It was in the contract."

He and Matthew exchanged quick glances. Matthew usually dealt with any contracts since Gerry could barely read, but Gerry signed this one upon receipt, not wanting to miss the opportunity.

"You can stay the night if you like," Chelsea continued. "That's in the contract, too."

Gerry pulled out his easy smile. "We didn't want to overstay our welcome, seeing as how we're just substitutes."

"Nonsense." She tapped his arm. "You did me a huge favor."

"Well, see you for that drink at two. Cheers."

Bridie's exhale hissed between her teeth as Chelsea walked away. "Why didn't you Charm her, ya eejit?"

"Charm her into opening the road just for us? You want to paint a target on the side of the caravan, too?"

"What are we going to do?"

"Stay," said Matthew. "And make the best of it."

Gerry nodded before turning a stern eye on me and Kai. "You stay backstage with us, yeah? No sneaking out to watch any shows."

I groaned in protest. It seemed a massive waste of time to be at a festival and not see any shows. Then it turned out the VIP pavilion was behind the main stage and had an open bar and endless food buffet. Kai and I got to watch the headliners from backstage, which was much better than being in the crowd. I also watched Gerry fend off Chelsea, expertly turning their drink into a party as he invited others to join them.

While Kai and I darted between the shows and hanging out with the other kids, our parents ate, drank, and jammed with their fellow musicians. All thought of Oren Kestrel evaporated, as if he no longer existed. When we returned to our caravan after the last show, our parents, all knackered, agreed this was the safest place to spend the night and we collapsed into our beds.

I awoke to the scent of bacon and eggs wafting through the open window next to my head. My stomach growled, and I pushed aside the curtain and climbed out of my bunk. The caravan was quiet, everyone still asleep, even Kai, with his bottomless stomach. I considered waking him, but I was weary of watching him all day yesterday. I wanted time on my own.

We'd stayed the night at festivals before, so I knew the drill. I even put on flannel pajamas the night before for the occasion. All I had to do was pull on a pair of trainers and I was good to go.

I slid out of our caravan quietly as possible and hiked across the parking lot/field. The festival site was humming with activity as work crews dismantled the structures. I reached the VIP pavilion where the party hadn't stopped. Half the people were standing around the bar, still in the same clothes as yesterday, while others were like me, in their pajamas and more intent on breakfast.

At the buffet, I loaded up on eggs, bacon, scones with plenty of lemon curd, and tea with plenty of cream. I sat at the end of one of the long tables and dug in. The canvas barriers between the VIP pavilion and the festival grounds had been removed and I could see the crew taking apart the main stage. They all wore flat caps, with colorful scarves knotted at their necks…

Shite.

Strowlers.

I swallowed the food I'd stopped chewing and took a sip of tea to force it down. I had to warn my family…

A man sat down across from me. He wore the cap and scarf, but unlike the crew, he sported a blue suit cut too tight, as if to show off his muscular frame. He had hard, blue eyes, a flat nose, small ears that stuck out, and a reddish-brown beard that was oddly unkempt, as if to hide his full lips. The morning sun glinted painfully off his bright gold watch and the thick rings studding his fingers.

I knew he was the Upright Man, head of the crew. My brain screamed scarper, but I didn't want to lead him to my family, so I stayed in place, heart pounding, not knowing what to do.

He sneered before saying, "So, you're the girl."

I didn't reply.

"I'm Oren Kestrel."

I froze, air caught in my chest. The actual Boogeyman of my childhood had me pinned in place.

"Mammy says you look just like Gerry." He shook his head. "There's naught of him in you."

What was that supposed to mean? I'd never met Gerry's mother. He must've sent her pictures, but why? All my life, I'd heard he'd been outcast from his Nest for walking the Wayward Way and being part of a Devil's Triangle.

"I know he's a molly. Everyone knows, no matter how hard he tries hiding behind that doxy and her gull."

My eyes widened. I couldn't let him trash my parents like that. I exhaled the breath I'd been holding and tried gathering courage with my next inhale, but he kept talking before I could speak.

"Did he tell you about our da? Doubt it. He wouldn't have the courage to say our father's name. It'd be a disgrace on his lips. Never mind that. Da built bombs for the IRA. Not for politics. He didn't give a toss about that. He just liked building bombs. Car bombs were his specialty. And like any good Strowler dad, he taught his oldest son the tricks of the trade, how to build and plant those bombs."

As he spoke, my heart started pounding so hard I could barely hear him. I wanted to run to my fathers, so they'd protect me, but I couldn't move. I couldn't lead him to my family. To Gerry.

"I tell you, it was a thing of beauty, watching a car explode." Oren smiled, his eyes lost for a moment in a distant memory. Then he laughed and made an explosion sound while mimicking the impact with his fingers splayed wide. "And knowing it was you what did some poor bastard in. That's power. I have that power." He leaned forward. I leaned back as far as I could without falling over. "The only reason there isn't a bomb planted in your caravan's engine is because of you and your brother. Even if you are bastards, you're still Sparrows and I don't need them coming at me for revenge. Tell Gerry this. Leave now and never return to Ulster. Using his whore's kids as human shields ends today. If he returns, he'll be sweating each time he turns the ignition on the caravan, because I won't care who's inside."

He winked, stood, and strutted away like a bantam cock, back toward the main stage and his crew.

I trembled so hard I had to grip the table to steady myself. He knew exactly where my family was. I had to warn them. I stood. My legs felt like rubber. I forced myself to walk and not run. I didn't want to give him that satisfaction. After I cleared the pavilion, my cramping stomach got the better of me. I ducked behind a moving van and bent over just as my breakfast came rushing out of my throat.

After I finished puking, I leaned against the van, taking deep breaths to steady myself. Then I ran all the way to our caravan.

My parents reacted as expected. Matthew wanted to find Oren and challenge him. Gerry declared he was sick and tired of living at Oren's beck and call. Bridie begged them to be sensible. While they fought, I crawled into my bunk and closed the curtain. Eventually, their voices quieted with their outrage. Even at 13, I knew we were outnumbered and outmaneuvered. Gerry and Matthew went outside to check the engine. When they finished, we were on the road in seconds.

I stared out the window, not taking an easy breath until we left Ulster.

Dream

PENNY

Gerry's dead. Why would Oren Kestrel lie about that?

Then again, why wouldn't he?

I want to be like Gareth, believing beyond hope that he's alive.

But I have these dreams.

Gerry lies atop his bed of jewels in the dragon's lair. His eyes are open and follow me as if trying to communicate, but he can't move, not even to blink. Master Stoorworm remains recumbent beside him, his fiery red gaze focused on both of us.

"Da," I say, "Is Oren telling the truth? Are you dead? Please, please tell me. Anything. Please."

His eyes close, but his mouth opens, and he starts singing Window in the Skies. His voice is breathy, as if it's taking everything to get the words out. Then the dragon thuds his front claw and the song ends.

Gerry remains still, so still, eyes and mouth closed, as if dead.

I wake up, fresh tears on my cheeks.

Window in the Skies.

Was he trying to tell me something about Gareth?

GERRY

It's hard not to be nervous, sitting in a pub, drinking a pint, and pretending to watch football while waiting for the love of your life.

Ten years, he'd said.

But a crisis in the Middle East allowed the military to prolong Gareth's service by another two, and he was gone the entire time. We'd talked regularly on video. Sometimes for hours. Sometimes for minutes if the situation there made him tense and terse. We'd been on-and-off lovers for years, me taking whatever scraps of time his schedule allowed.

During the off times, I followed my fancy, casually, cautiously, never with love. That was reserved for him and my family. It was hard at first, after Bridie and Matthew got together. I wondered what the point of me was and if I shouldn't make our lives easier and scarper, but I couldn't leave my daughter. They were willing to walk the Wayward Way with me and take the shame that came from being in a Devil's Triangle. I became a father again after Kai was born. This family became my true family. The Ulster Kestrel Nest was a distant nightmare until Oren woke me up by threatening my daughter.

After that, I kept my fancy to myself. It was months before I stopped checking the caravan engine before turning the ignition. Oren's face haunted my dreams, just as it had when I was a kid, sleeping anywhere that kept him from finding me. I had this fear, secret, never to be shared, that if he got me alone, he'd do what he'd done to me as a child, and then kill me.

Sometimes, I wonder if that's the only reason I'm still alive, because he wants one last go at me.

We spent the last year traveling the continent, mostly in Italy, playing in pubs that welcome an authentic Irish band. We had a cozy domestic life. I refurbished scooters while Matthew gave the kids an education and Bridie kept house. We stayed clear of other Strowlers and the judgment that came with them. It would've been idyllic if I wasn't so damn lonely, pining for the one thing I couldn't have. Contact with Gareth had petered out to nothing. He wasn't returning my calls or texts. I'd have thought the worst if his sister hadn't assured me he was still alive.

We were in Rome, playing a week-long gig at a pub called Fiddler's Green, when we got word Helena had been elected Mad Maud, Chief of the London Beggar Clan. She asked us to attend her inauguration and perform for the party afterward. Adults only, to the great disappointment of our children, but how could we say no?

We'd been back in London two days when I got a text from Gareth.

A bloody text.

Gareth: Meet me at the Star and Plough?

That bloody bastard.

I swore a blue streak at the phone before shoving it in my pocket and going back to work on a Vespa. That lasted a hot minute before I pulled the phone back out.

Gerry: Sure, mate. When?

Gareth: 2:30

I gave a thumbs up. Then I hurried into the caravan to take a shower. I put on a pair of jeans, a T-shirt, and a hoodie, and headed out the door. And came right back in and changed my outfit to leather pants, a maroon shirt, and my tight, brown leather jacket.

If I'm being dumped, I'll do it in style.

What else could it be? Why would he contact me like that if not to tell me it was over, that he'd found someone else? What a bastard move, though, breaking up with me in the pub where we first met.

My family observed in bemused silence. Finally, Penny chirped, "Where you off to, Da?"

"Nowhere special, love." I patted her cheek. At least I'd always have her, my rock, my reason for being.

I was determined to arrive fashionably late, but instead of meandering through the streets on my scooter, I made a beeline for the pub, arriving 15 minutes early.

I'm such a gom.

Now I'm waiting, the stool beneath me literally pins and needles. I don't fancy sport, but I stare at the telly so I don't stare at the door. The other punters are pounding the bar, hooting and whistling over the movement of a ball. The sound is off, and the speakers are broadcasting the usual Irish bands.

U2's Window in the Skies comes on and I mutter, "Bugger." I don't need to hear a song about eternal love. Maybe I should wait outside.

Then I hear the tap of a cane behind me. I feel him. His heat, his strength, his goodness. I swivel on my stool.

Gareth stands before me, leaning heavily on that cane. His jeans and T-shirt hang loose on his lanky frame, as if he's lost two stone, and his sparse beard doesn't fill his hollow cheeks. The left side of his face and neck is one solid, faded bruise. Those blue eyes stare at me, sad and haunted, expecting rejection.

Tears fill my eyes as I slide off the stool and fold him into my embrace. His free arm slides around my waist and he leans heavily on me, his forehead pressed to my shoulder. Then he lifts his head and my eyes close as our lips touch.

Our kiss… it's as if my soul has melted into his. All that exists in this moment are me, and him, and Bono's voice singing of a love that hurts, nearly destroys, but leaves a window in the skies.

This is our window. It's wide open and I'm climbing in.

His lips, tongue, scent are as I remember. Two years are a long time to go without your heart's deepest desire. Then a hooting sound interrupts our bliss. Hands thump the bar, hard. I break our kiss and spin around.

The punters shout, "Goooooooal!"

I exhale. The madness of love, that I'd kiss my love in a public bar, in full view of anyone. There must be some magic to this place, that these particular punters don't care. I let go of Gareth and lean over the bar to order two pints.

Shane's son, Ian, tends the bar in the afternoon. When I hold a tenner, he nods at Gareth and asks, "He a soldier?"

I nod.

"On the house, mate."

"Cheers."

This magic, I don't know how long it will last. I lead Gareth to that corner where we shared our first pint all those years ago, when I spilled my baby gay guts to him. I want to keep this bubble around us for as long as it will last.

Gareth waves away my offer of help and slides into his chair with a pained grunt. He leans his cane against the wall, takes up his glass and clinks it against mine. His eyes close with bliss as he takes a long sip. "Ah, god, I missed this."

"You know what I missed? You. What the hell happened? Were you unconscious? Why didn't Helena tell me?"

"Don't blame her. I told her not to tell anyone."

"But why? What happened?"

"Missile strike hit our hospital. I... I..." He gives a dry chuckle. "I don't know how I'm still alive. Anyway, they saved my leg, but had to replace the hip. After that, they discharged me home. I didn't... I couldn't talk to anyone. Not even Helena. I just..." He shakes his head. "Went inside myself. It wasn't until she told me she'd been elected Beggar Chief that I finally felt something. I was so damn proud of her. I wanted to feel happy again, and I wanted to share that happiness with you."

I duck my head as tears rush back to my eyes. "I wish you'd told me, but I understand. Not what you went through. I mean, not being able to talk about something terrible that happened to you." I pause. My experience with Oren almost slips from my lips, but I bite it back. This isn't the time or place. Maybe it never will be. "I thought you were going to tell me you'd found someone else."

Gareth grins, a sparkle of joy in his eyes. "You mad bastard. Who else is there?"

"You tell me, mate."

"There's no one else. There's only you. If this taught me anything, it's that I don't want to waste any more time. I want to make a go of it, Gerry. You and me. If you're willing."

"Are you asking me to marry you?"

"Yes. I can't get down on one knee."

"I don't need that. All I need is you. Yes. Even though I don't know how it's going to work. You're Glory Road. I'm Wayward Way. You're stuck in London. I travel. And I can't leave my family. Not the kids, at least. Not until they're grown."

"We'll find a way to make it work. I can't leave the Beggar Clan yet, not with Helena's election. Let's take it as it comes right now and eventually, when the times right, I'll join you."

"On the road, in our own caravan, on the Wayward Way?" I whisper as if saying it aloud will make it disappear.

"As long as I can be with you, wherever that is."

Our hands clasp under the table. I know I won't be going home tonight. I don't want to rush it. Things still need to be said. I reach for my drink and drain half the glass to loosen the hold on my tongue. "If you're with me, you put a target on your back."

Gareth scoffs. "You think Oren's going to touch me? I'm the Beggar Chief's brother. He looks at me wrong and all the Beggars in Ulster will have a go at him. There's never been a better time for us, Gerry."

He's right. This is it. I somehow lucked into powerful friends and a man who loves me. I'd be a fool to let Oren run or ruin the rest of my life.

But I'd also be a fool if I believe Oren is done with me.

Dream

GERRY

"How did I die?" I ask that damn dragon for the thousandth time.

He doesn't answer or even stir from his bejeweled nest. Maybe he's asleep.

Maybe I can scarper.

I will my body to move, even the tiniest motion, the twitch of a finger, but nothing. Am I paralyzed or in a coma or both? My heartbeat quickens at that thought.

I have a heartbeat.

I'm alive!

Or is this all an illusion?

Did I die or am I still dreaming?

I close my eyes and go over everything that happened up to finding myself here, in a dragon's lair.

I'm with Matthew. We leave the pub and get into a car that our client sent…

Matthew.

He's falling as if pushed out a window.

I'm falling, too.

We're falling together.

No, he can't die. Bridie will be lost without him.

I twist around so my body takes the impact as we hit the ground…

Nothing. I don't feel my head crack or my back break. It's as though my soul left my body, but here I am. My heart is still beating.

Thud.

Thud.

Thud.

"Is Matthew dead, too?" I call out.

The dragon ignores me.

Matthew, dead. My best mate. My partner in crime. It can't be. Bridie. The kids. Who will look after them? Tears stream from my eyes. How, if I'm dead?

I think, hard as I can, but I can't remember anything beyond that. Was our client a sham - a trick to flush me out, make me vulnerable and end me, and Matthew with me? Who would do that? Only one name comes to mind.

Oren.

He must've heard about me and Gareth, and decided to act. He couldn't take out Bridie and the kids since they're Sparrows. Why risk killing Matthew? Does he think the Two Dragon Clan will look the other way? Maybe that's his cover. Matthew's death takes some of the suspicion off him. Makes him free to pursue his next target…

Gareth.

I must do something. I must stop him, but how? What do I have left, but my ability to annoy a dragon?

That's it.

"Oy," I call out. "Oy, mate. You want me to shut my gob, yeah?"

He doesn't reply, but I can tell by the perk of his horns that he's listening.

"Look, I'll cooperate. Do whatever you please. Die, if that's what's going on here, if I'm still alive somehow. Or if I'm haunting you, I'll stop that, yeah? I'll do whatever you want. I need you to protect Gareth from Oren."

Master Stoorworm's sides expand as if in a massive sigh. I feel the heat of his sulfurous breath. He makes a scuttling motion, coins and jewels scattering in all directions as he slithers out of the cave.

Where is he going? To save Gareth? To get away from me because I won't shut up? Both? Neither?

"Help him, you manky fuck. I'll do anything. You hear me? Anything!"

The next thing I know, I'm looking through my daughter's eyes. She's standing outside the Beggar's Abode, searching for someone. For Gareth. I need to warn her, but how?

What will this dragon allow?

Present

PENNY

I don't dream of Gerry, or Matthew, or even the dragon. Oren Kestrel haunts my sleep with his vicious eyes and harsh voice demanding some strange vengeance. I awaken abruptly, shivering, and press the pillow to my mouth so I don't scream.

After I calm down, I think about those dreams. There was grief in that fury of his, as if he mourned the loss in Gerry in some perverse way that could only lead to violence and death.

I scrub my eyes with the heels of my hands. It's ridiculous. It was a dream, or rather a nightmare. And yet, I can't shake the feeling that Oren didn't kill Gerry and Matthew.

All these dreams mean nothing. I need to face reality. After I spoke to Oren, Helena called Eddie Lark. He confirmed that Gerry's body was dumped in front of the London Nest, and Oren had retrieved it.

Da is dead, his ashes spread at the crossroads, and there's nothing we can do about it.

I get up and haul Kai out of bed. We go to the common room for breakfast and bring back food for Bridie, which she refuses before going back to sleep. I turn on telly and find an episode of Doctor Who we haven't seen. I can't focus on the Doctor's antics, but I pretend to for Kai's sake. He watches, unsmiling, and I wonder if he's doing the same for me.

There's a knock on the door. Then it slides open, and Helena walks in, her face pinched with worry. "I'm sorry to barge in, but Gareth is missing. Have you seen him?"

I shake my head, mute with sudden fear. I pull out my phone to check for messages, but there are none.

She gives a tight huff. "I texted him about an hour ago and he told me to leave him alone. It's probably fine. I'm worried something might have happened. Or that's he's gone some-where…" She gives us a furtive glance.

"You mean gone to see Oren?" I ask.

Helena nods reluctantly. "I have eyes on the London Nest, and Gareth hasn't been seen. It's probably nothing." She glances at the bedroom door. "Is your mother awake?" We shake our heads. She sighs. "Let me know if you hear from him."

We nod and she leaves. I wait a few minutes before putting on my shoes and grabbing my jacket.

"Are you going to find Pa?" asks Kai.

I nod.

"Take me with you."

"I can't. If something happens to me, you need to be here for Mum."

His eyes widen. "Don't go."

"I have to, for Da's sake. I need to make sure Pa is all right. Don't leave Mum until I get back, yeah?"

He doesn't reply. His forlorn little face reproaches me as I leave the car.

I'm pretty sure I know where Gareth is. Should I tell Helena? If he's where I think, then he's in no danger and doesn't want to be bothered. The Abode is a literal hive. If he needed some place private to mourn, it wouldn't be here.

As I take the lift to the street level, I think about how to make a break for it. The guards will stop me at the front entrance and call Helena. I could Charm my way through if my parents hadn't been so adamant about my age. Fine. I don't have Charm, but I can sham as well as any Strowler.

The Beggars turned the front of Greycoat Station into a homeless advocacy group called the Hearth. They provide three hot meals a day, plus counseling. It's the perfect cover, as the Beggars blend in perfectly with clientele, coming and going as they please.

I take a deep breath before sauntering across the corridor to the large metal gate blocking the entrance to the Abode. Neither guard looks familiar. I cross my fingers, hoping they mistake me for a Beggar kid.

"Hi, I'm looking for my mum," I say, casual-like. "She's supposed to be talking to one of the counselors. Do you mind if I go check?"

"Who's your mum?" asks the guard to my left.

"Mavis Abram. We're new, assigned here from the Watford Abode."

They exchange glances and shrugs. As the guard slides open the door, she says, "Stay clear of the clients and come right back."

I nod in reply, not wanting to risk a wrong word. Then I head for the cubicles that house the counselors. It's my lucky day. Homeless clients pack the lobby, waiting their turn for food or advice. I crane my neck, peering around as if searching for my mother. Then I glance back at the guards. They're busy with a group of Beggars reentering the station. I slip through the front entrance, easy as you please, and out to the streets of London.

I blink rapidly, my eyes unaccustomed to the sun after a week below. It's also warmer than the perpetual chill of the tunnels, but I'm not bothered to take off my jacket. I need to find Gareth before Helena realizes I've scarpered.

As I scurry down the street, I think about what I'll say to Gareth. I doubt he'll welcome my intrusion, but maybe more than anyone else's. I'll apologize and suggest he call his sister and then hurry back to the Abode before I'm missed.

I'm about a block away from my destination when my phone buzzes. I pull it out of my pocket and grind to a halt as I look at the name on the screen.

Penny.

I sent myself a text, except I didn't. Was I hacked? I hesitate before tapping to open the message.

It's a gif of an exploding car.

I freeze.

Then I shriek and set off at a run.

I cross the street without looking and hear the squeal of a car slamming on its brakes. Horns honk, but I ignore them as I enter the alley with the red brick buildings. I rush to the end of the parking lot, but my pace slows to a halt when I see a green Mini Cooper instead of a black Volvo in Gareth's spot.

Am I on the wrong street? I spin around and everything looks right, from the buildings to the peeling stickers on the blue and gray rubbish bins.

I pant, pressing my hand to my pounding heart. No, no, no. Someone took his spot. Maybe he parked somewhere nearby, but where? How can I find him in all of London? I need to call Helena.

Before I can reach for my phone, I hear something. The whisper of a whisper.

Listen, Penny, listen.

It feels like Gerry.

"Da?" I breathe out.

Listen.

I feel compelled to walk, slowly at first, before hurrying out of the alley and back into the street. Then compelled to stop.

Listen.

It takes a moment, but then I hear it. So faint. A song of love, loss, and redemption. But how do I follow such a sound? My feet move again of their own accord. I scurry across two streets, dodging past people who scoff their annoyance. The song becomes louder as I enter an alley with brownstone buildings and spot a black Volvo parked beside a pair of blue rubbish bins. The window is unrolled, and Gareth sits with his head bowed over the steering wheel while listening to Window in the Skies.

"Gareth," I call out, which startles both him and me. I've only ever called him Uncle Gareth or Pa. "Gerry wants you to know that he'll love you forever. Never doubt it."

He wipes at the tears streaming down his pale cheeks. "But he's gone."

"No. He's still here." Is he? Did I imagine his voice? How else did I wind up here? I can't say that to Gareth. I press my hand against my chest. "In our hearts. He'll never die."

Gareth looks at me as though he knows I'm trying to help and failing miserably. "Look, love, I don't know how you found me, but…"

I hold up my hands. "No, Pa. Don't touch anything. Don't move. You're in danger."

"What are you talking about?"

"Oren Kestrel. I think he planted a bomb in your car."

Gareth freezes. I whip out my phone and call Helena. Within minutes, the Beggar Clan arrives with a military grade bomb squad. Beggars disguised as police hold off curious bystanders. Helena orders me to leave. I go to the end of the alley and wait, watching, until they extract Gareth from the Volvo.

I run to him, throwing myself into his arms. As we embrace, he whispers, "Did Gerry tell you?"

"I don't know how, but, yes," I whisper back. Then I turn to his sister, watching us with a grim frown. "Is there a bomb?"

"Yes. How did you know?"

I show her the gif. "Someone hacked my phone."

"Oren Kestrel?"

I can't tell her my dead father sent me a gif. "Maybe. But why would he warn me?"

"That bastard's a sadist," snaps Gareth. "It's no fun for him unless everyone is suffering."

That's true enough. Maybe he was the one who sent it. But why me? Does he hate me that much? And if he does, what does that bode for my family?

"Right," says Helena crisply. "I'm calling Eddie Lark and demanding he turn Oren Kestrel over to me. The Strowlers owe their existence in London to our benevolence. I won't allow this challenge to my authority go unpunished."

I stand apart from them, hugging myself, a Strowler. What will be the fallout for me and my family?

"We have to leave, that's all there is to it," Bridie states dully as she packs, cramming rather than neatly folding her clothes.

"Why?" I demand, my arms folded and my suitcase empty.

"Because that's what was negotiated between Eddie Lark and Mad Maud."

"I know that. They're on the Glory Road. We're on the Wayward Way. We don't have to listen to them."

"We can't stay in the Abode. We're not Beggars."

"We'll stay in our caravan."

"How? Gerry and Matthew were the breadwinners. Without them, we're skint."

I scoff and kick the bed. Bridie huffs out a long, sad sigh before sitting on the mattress and patting the spot beside her. I don't move. She sighs again. "You know the terms of their agreement. Oren Kestrel will be banished from London for the rest of his life if we return to the Sparrow Nest."

"But why? Why do they want us to do that?"

"It's a matter of honor. Taking refuge with the Beggar Clan means we don't trust our own people."

"We don't."

"Not trusting them dishonors them, and honor is everything on the Crossroads, especially for the Glory Road lot." Her hands fold in her lap and her face creases with grief. "I didn't tell Helena and Gareth because I don't want to hurt them more, but Eddie Lark has also demanded that we cut all contact with them."

"No." I shake my head vehemently. "Absolutely not. We don't have to listen to him."

"We do, at least for the time being. If we don't, then Oren is free to return to London and finish what he started with Gareth. Look, we don't even know who killed your fathers or why. Staying here makes him a target. If we go back to our Nest, he'll be safe and so will we."

"So, we just cut him off without a word?"

"We wait until we're in the Nest and I'll explain to him and Helena as best I can."

"Why not tell them now?"

"Because I'm not strong enough, not if I look at their faces. Now, start packing."

I do as Bridie did, angrily cramming my clothes into my suitcase. Last to be packed is the green dress I wore the night my fathers died. I clutch it to my chest, allowing the tears to spill down my cheeks. This can't be it. I won't let it be.

Da, are you there? What should I do?

I reach out mentally, trying desperately to sense Gerry's presence, but also hoping I don't. If his ashes are spread at the crossroads, then he'll never rest. I wait, breathless. Nothing. He's gone.

I fold the green dress and carefully pack it away. It's time to play the long game. Cooperate for now until the time comes.

I will return to London, and I will find out who murdered my fathers.

Dream

GERRY

The dragon allows me to see through my daughter's eyes until the man I love is safe.

To know through her that Matthew is dead.

And that no one knows who killed us.

I mean, aside from the obvious suspect.

"Did Oren kill me?" I ask the dragon. "Does he bear the Mark of Cain?"

Master Stoorworm's eyes open as he shifts on his mountain of Spanish doubloons. Gold coins cascade with his movement. "All humans are capable of murder."

"And you lot aren't?"

"Dragons don't kill each other." His lipless mouth curls in what looks like a smirk. Smug bastard. His head settles back on his claws. His lids slide over his eyes, the translucent one before the scaled one. "Rest. Sleep. Dream."

A bargain's a bargain. I said I'd cooperate, and I will. Is this death? Endless dreams? If that's the case, I'll choose to dream what I will, of a family too good for this world and a love burned into my soul.

And when that manky prick's not looking, somehow, I'll find my way back to my family.

The story continues in Fake: Dragons of the Crossroads Book 1. Determined to put the Crossroads behind her, Bridie marries a Bleater and moves with her children to San Francisco. Penny hates her new, fake life and is determined to return to London and solve the mystery of her fathers' murders. Then she meets a mysterious orphan named Lennon, who's also on a quest for vengeance. The two teens form an unlikely alliance, but will their growing love seal their doom?

To find out more about Dragons of the Crossroads and to purchase more books in the series, please go to loriwriter.com.

<h1 style="font-family:cursive">Acknowledgments</h1>

Heartfelt thanks to Jennifer Gagliardi, India Cale, and Andy Pettit for their contributions to this book.

About the Author

Lori Saltis left her heart in San Francisco. She goes to visit it whenever she can afford the bridge toll. She's been an indie author since 2016. She's very passionate about the themes of alienation and found family. Her favorite genre is fantasy because who doesn't want to believe they'll look up in the sky one day and see a dragon?

To find out more about the world of the Crossroads, check out her website loriwriter.com.